Death's Good Dog
An Aztec West Novella

Death's Good Dog
An Aztec West Novella

TL Morganfield

FSB

DEATH'S GOOD DOG
AN AZTEC WEST NOVELLA

copyright © 2015 by T.L. Morganfield

Cover design by TL Morganfield

This story is a work of fiction. Names, characters, places, and events in this book either are products of the author's imagination or are used fictitiously. Any resemblance to actual events, places, or persons living or dead, is purely coincidental.

All Rights Reserved, including the right to reproduce this book, or portions thereof, in any form whatsoever.

Published by Feathered Serpent Books
Thornton, Colorado

Printed in the USA

ISBN 978-0-9909207-4-8

For Daisy, Tigger, Buddy, Calvin, Jake, Fiona, and Lily: all of the good dogs that have enriched my life through the years.

Sometimes when he arrived at the gates of the underworld, Xolotl would find a recently deceased soul waiting for him; there'd been times hundreds of years ago when lines of people had been waiting, all anxious to begin the treacherous journey to eternal peace, but those days were long over. Most humans worshipped different gods now.

But Xolotl didn't expect to see two archangels waiting for him. Raphael's presence—while rare—wasn't entirely unexpected, for he was the warden of the various underworlds, but seeing Michael dressed in his shimmering gold armor and looming on the stone stairs like an emerald-winged albatross was never a good sign. Xolotl tried to duck into a nearby alcove, hoping they hadn't seen him yet, but he was too slow. "Xolotl!" Michael boomed.

Xolotl cringed but hurried out onto the stairs again, morphing from his dog-form to his twisted, hunched human one, so he could bow, as expected. "Greetings, My Lord." He fixed his one-eyed gaze on his own backward-pointing feet.

Michael came down to him. "Couldn't you at least summon cleaner clothing than that rag you call a loincloth?"

"I must conserve my magic, My Lord, for it's difficult to renew." Xolotl didn't dare look up.

Michael guffawed. "And yet there's always enough magic to change into that mangy dog, so you can blend in topside. What do you do up there, anyway?"

Xolotl hesitated a breath before answering, "I enjoy the sunlight, My Lord. Mictlan is dark and cold, and with no one left to lead through the trials, time can be...dreary."

The archangel pushed past, nearly sprawling Xolotl with his wings. "I wish to see your master."

"Of course. Lord Death always welcomes your visits, My Lord." Xolotl turned to leave.

But Raphael's outspread golden-brown wings blocked any means of slipping by. "The Archangel will travel the road today and, as its guardian, he will require your services." He held his hand out, motioning Xolotl back down the stairs.

"But only death gods can walk the road without turning mortal," Xolotl said, startled.

"I'm well aware of the rules, Black Dog," Michael barked. "Now come along."

Xolotl cast one last questioning gaze up at Raphael—which was met with an impatient eyebrow raise—then he started back down the stairs, his shoulders sagging. He'd been looking forward to his trip to the surface. When he wasn't watching his own awkward feet on the steps, he stared at the oddly-angled set of Michael's right wing: evidence of a battle he'd nearly lost three hundred years ago. If he didn't hate Michael so much, he might have pitied him; his wings had been rather beautiful before the Smoking Mirror got hold of them.

The stairs ended at a stone balcony overlooking a bottomless chasm. An archway to the left led into another cavern and the angels had to stretch their wings behind them to squeeze through. Xolotl turned back into his dog-form before trotting into the first cavern of the underworld.

"What happened to all of that talk of conserving magic?" Michael asked.

"This makes the road easier for me, My Lord," Xolotl said. "I presume you wish to make the trip as quickly as possible?" But the question only garnered a grunt.

The cavern's ceiling was lost to the darkness above. A river of black water ran along the right side, disappearing into the wall next to the doorway, and Xolotl's dim mud-and-thatch hut sat opposite it, under the gnarled branches of a dead copal tree, surrounded by tall patches of sharp grasses. A pile of dried bones spilled out the doorway—the remains of the sacrifices the humans once gave to thank him for leading their departed loved ones through the trials to their final rest in oblivion. Several small dog skulls grinned out from the mess.

Ghost lights dotted the air like fireflies, and a few floated closer as the angels approached the edge of the river, but they scattered like startled rabbits when Michael flapped his wings at them. "Get out of here and go warn your master that I'm coming!" he called after them as they disappeared one after another into the body of the copal tree. He shook his wings and ruffled his feathers, looking distinctly ill-tempered. "Let's hurry up then," he muttered to Raphael. "Things change fast in the human world these days."

"Are you sure you want *him* here when we do this?" Raphael asked, tipping his head toward Xolotl. "I can do the survey myself—"

"No, I want to do it, and Lord Death will need to speak with the cripple once we've finished." He sneered at Xolotl. "Time is of the essence."

Then why don't you just apparate into Mictlan, you vulture, Xolotl thought. But only a fool would make the suggestion aloud, and while many considered both Xolotl and his master cowards, only the stupid considered them fools.

Raphael nodded, but when he spoke next, he lowered his voice. "You'll be easier to carry if you put away your wings, Brother."

"Very well." Michael sighed, but when he noticed

Xolotl watching them, he snapped, "Go swim your stupid river, Black Dog. We'll be along in a moment."

Xolotl bowed his head in deference—the better to mutter under his breath unseen—then he turned to the river. Before stepping in though, he chanced a glance over his shoulder at the angels.

Michael's wings were gone, leaving him looking small and quite human. He let Raphael hook his arms underneath his own and then lock his hands together across his sternum. Raphael then rose into the air slowly, beating his wings hard against Michael's added weight. Soon he carried the Archangel across the broad cavern, past the river and into the cavern beyond.

Xolotl stared a moment, letting the sight sink in. He'd only seen Michael a handful of times since the Conquest—and always walking upon the ground—so it baffled him to see that the Archangel couldn't fly anymore.

The souls of humans who'd died on the Eagle Stone went to the heaven of whatever god they fed with their sacrifice, but those who died peacefully in their beds used to face nine trials to reach Mictlan, to prove their worth to Lord Death. They had to cross an open plain where it rained arrowheads and climb a mountain of obsidian blades. There were vicious snakes to slay, a river with weeds that felt like hands reaching up to pull one under, and a gauntlet of flaming flags that scorched flesh to the bone.

By the time most humans reached Lord Death's Eagle Stone—where they had to cut out their own heart in sacrifice to him—they were all too eager to do whatever was necessary to make the torture stop.

Xolotl's job—the entire reason he existed at all—was to lead the dead through those trials, and keep them motivated to reach the end and claim their reward. He hadn't done it in at least fifty years, maybe even seventy-five, and he couldn't remember having ever walked the road without leading someone—be they living or dead. He'd long ago learned all the easy paths and shortcuts, and his death-god magic shielded him from the inevitable physical harms the road brought, so it wasn't an arduous journey.

But Raphael and Michael avoided all this by flying over, scouting around like a pair of explorers charting the boundaries of their country's new territory. It made Xolotl uneasy.

After coming down the mudslides, Xolotl trotted across the dusty gray plain stretching endlessly into the distance. A faint fog slid around him like apparitions, turning everything white. In the distance, the waters of the Black Lake lapped against its shores.

When the angels finally landed, Raphael's massive wings scattered the fog enough to see the rubble of Lord Death's Eagle Stone. Just as the humans had vandalized the temples above ground, the angels had broken this one with their flaming swords when they took over. Centuries-old blood still blackened the ground around it, and Michael spared it a disgusted glance as he shrugged himself free of Raphael's arms. "I want to see the others first," he said, jaw tight with frustration.

"Of course, Archangel." Xolotl led them until the fog gave way. Lord Death's palace of obsidian and bone sat to the north of the Black Lake, surrounded by fields of reeds. More ghost lights hovered like wisps of cottonwood, many fleeing towards the palace as the three immortals stepped from the fog. The remainder took refuge in the clusters of naked copal trees hunched over the water.

At least fifty dim figures sat around the banks, all staring out over the dark water, unmoving. They varied in size and shape, some male, some female, some neither or even both; some looked rather human while others were a mishmash of man and monster; some wore ornate clothing and jewelry while others—like the god Paynal—wore only their bones. In this gloomy circle sat what remained of the fierce and merciless gods who once ruled the land now known as Mexico.

"Resting peacefully, I see." Michael's voice boomed in the silence. He bent down in front of Tlaloc, scrutinizing the rain god's tusk-like fangs and the stone goggles encircling his tiny, shriveled eyes. Setting his palm against the god's forehead, he pushed, sending Tlaloc tipping slowly backwards until his limp body sprawled upon the ground. The shadow of a satisfied smile crossing his face, he went to the next in line—the love goddess Xochiquetzal—and did the same. He repeated the process god by god, his expression growing more gleeful each time.

But the joy vanished when he came to Smoking Mirror.

Death's Good Dog

The dark sorcerer god stared back, his obsidian-mirror eyes unblinking, a hint of a smile on his handsome yet cruel human face. Michael didn't touch him at first, just stared, the brooding anger growing hotter in his gaze.

Then suddenly he lashed out, kicking Smoking Mirror hard enough to crush bone, if the god had any. But Smoking Mirror lay perfectly still, blissfully unaware of anything. Michael wrenched his limp body off the ground and made to throw it into the lake.

But Raphael stepped in front of him. "Remember what Father said."

Michael glared at Raphael but then tossed Smoking Mirror back onto the ground. He ruffled his bad wing then spat on the motionless body, breathing heavily.

Xolotl had followed behind Michael in his twisted human form, setting each god back upright, but when he went to Smoking Mirror, Michael kicked him aside.

With a yelp, Xolotl went over backwards into the water, dropping like a stone over a cliff. Like the chasm off the ledge outside his house, the lake was bottomless, and it wasn't long at all before he was submerged in utter darkness. To fall too far was absolute death for a god, so he paddled frantically with his deformed limbs but kept sinking. He nearly panicked before remembering his dog-form was better for such activities, so he changed. He still struggled against the eternal pull below him but eventually he broke the surface.

A pair of strong hands dragged him ashore, drenched. "Are you all right?" To his surprise, it was Raphael's voice.

"Of course he's all right. He's alive, and he can swim,"

Michael said. "Now let's get going. I have much to discuss with Lord Death."

Xolotl cast a grudging glare at Michael's back as the angel started off towards the palace. *Someday you'll get yours, Michael.* He turned away when Raphael narrowed his eyes at him though. *Someday....*

Lord Death knew they were coming; his ghost light sentinels informed him of all that transpired in his realm. He greeted Michael at the palace gate, his careful smile and regal demeanor betraying his nervousness. He was an extraordinarily tall god—towering even over the hulking war god Mextli—but his body was little more than bones. The twin ghost lights hovering in his hollow eye sockets gave the translucent skin covering his skull a pale, deathly-blue glow, and he wore a robe and crown of brown owl feathers and a necklace of tiny animal skulls. He used to wear a garland of extruded eyeballs, but Michael had proclaimed it an abomination and threw it into the Black Lake.

"It's always a pleasure to welcome you into my realm, Archangel," Lord Death said with a bow, his bones creaking. "To what do I owe the pleasure of your visit?"

Michael shouldered past him. "We have important business to discuss." When Xolotl started following them inside, Michael snapped, "This doesn't concern witless minor gods, Black Dog. Wait outside and your master will explain everything to you later, in small, easy to understand words."

Xolotl blinked, taken aback. He was used to the insults to his intelligence, but as Lord Death's assistant, anything that affected the realm was his concern as well. As expected, Raphael glared at him then followed Michael into the palace.

But when Xolotl gazed imploringly at Lord Death, his master pointed him away. "Go already." When Xolotl glared at the angels' backs, Lord Death added, "Away with you, or you'll get kicked."

Xolotl finally trotted away, his nape bristling. *I don't know what I was thinking. Lord Death never stands up for me, not even to angels.*

Once the palace doors creaked shut, he grumbled, "You're the witless one, Michael." At a quick trot, he headed for the cenote opposite the palace.

He descended the stone path leading down to the water. "I might not be a brilliant war strategist like Mextli, or understand anything of the mathematics Quetzalcoatl came up with to figure the earthly seasons, but I know everything there is to know about death! Ha! I even know things *I shouldn't*." He sat at the edge of the water and stared at himself in the still, quicksilver surface. His wolf-like face peered back at him, one-eyed and ferocious, but it soon vanished, replaced with a twisted, mournful human one as he returned to his natural form. His long hair hung around his greenish, corpse-like face in wet, matted clumps. "I'm not stupid," he murmured, the anger replaced with melancholy.

"Who called you stupid?" a voice asked from the

darkness of the nearby cave.

When he jumped to his twisted feet and looked over his shoulder, a woman stepped out of the shadows. His face heated. "Oh, Lady Death, I wasn't expecting you out here." When she glanced up towards the lip of the cenote, he quickly added, "Don't worry, I won't tell the master you were out here." She had strict orders from Lord Death to always remain further back in the caves.

"Will you come sit with me?" she asked, retreating back into the shadows again. "I'll make you something to eat."

"Of course, My Lady."

Xolotl followed her through dark passages deep into the caverns, until they reached a little stone archway guarded by a ghost light. She held the door curtain aside for him.

Blue fire burned in the hearth, casting a cold glow on the odd trinkets and furnishings rarely seen in the houses of gods. A loom with a half-finished tapestry sat next to a bed roll and a metlatl grinding stone. The smell of freshly cooked tortillas filled the air. A thick slab of wood served as a table in front of the fire, with two reed mats for sitting on.

"Would you like one?" Lady Death asked Xolotl as she unwrapped a linen cloth, revealing the source of the pleasant aroma. "I'll put bugs in it for you."

"Thank you." Xolotl sat on one of the reed mats.

She poured live insects from a clay jar into the center of the tortilla then quickly wrapped it closed, sealing the ends to prevent any escapes. When she handed it to him, he took it down in three massive bites. These days he relied exclusively on these insects to rejuvenate his magic;

whatever surface Lord Death touched, centipedes and beetles would burst forth, carrying tiny bits of his magic inside them.

Lady Death sat on the other mat. "Was the master saying nasty things about you again?"

"No. I was just...venting."

She smiled. "I don't think you're stupid. And anyone who says you are is a fool."

The flush crept up his neck. Her name was Lady Death, but she bore no resemblance to her husband. She looked more like a very beautiful woman who'd been plucked off the earth, blessed with magic and given a gown of owl feathers. She was unfailingly kind and never lacked for a smile, but best of all, Xolotl never had to be on guard with her; she never criticized or belittled, and she made the underworld a little brighter.

But with every bit of his being, Xolotl was sure she belonged in the sunlight, not locked up in the shadows; a feeling made stronger by virtue that he couldn't remember having known her prior to the angel's conquest. It was as if those memories had been erased.

"I thought you were going to spend some time in the sun," she said, a hint of longing in her voice.

Xolotl nodded. "I was, but then I met Michael on the stairs—"

The soothing smile faded from her face. "Michael's here? Why?"

"He's talking to the master."

"About what?"

He shrugged. "He said I was too witless to sit in on the

meeting."

"Never mind any of them." She still furrowed her brows, bothered, but then she let a smile soften her face. "Tell me again about how things are up on the surface now."

He much preferred these kinds of conversations. It helped them both forget the dreariness of the underworld for a while. "Remember how the Mexicans rebelled against their overlords in Spain? Well, now they've gotten themselves into their first war, with the people of the north."

"The Americans?" When Xolotl nodded, she asked, "What for?"

"Who understands the motivations of humanity anymore? I'm sure it has something to do with gold and land and religion; it always does. And there's been much shouting about Manifest Destiny."

"What's that?"

"I don't know. But many Americans are moving into Aztlan, heading to some place they call California. I haven't been there myself, so I haven't any idea what all the fuss is about."

Lady Death nodded, melancholy on her face. "The world changes so fast now, doesn't it?"

"Too fast," Xolotl conceded. "First the Spanish with their muskets and horses, and now...the humans are building things that move as if alive but they have no mind or spirit. They call them Iron Horses, for they move as fast as the beasts, but they never tire. They belch fire and cover everything in black soot. Not even Quetzalcoatl himself predicted such things."

"No, I don't suppose he did." Her sadness grew still deeper. That always happened when he mentioned the Feathered Serpent.

Not all of the gods had ended up on the banks of the Black Lake; some still managed to elude the angels even today, and Quetzalcoatl was one of them. Lord Death saw it as proof of treachery; Xolotl himself was unsure. "Do you think it's true? That Quetzalcoatl betrayed us to the angels and now he lives with them in Omeyocan?"

Lady Death's expression darkened. "The Feathered Serpent is many things, but not a traitor."

Xolotl snorted then looked away. "I used to believe that too, but if he really cared about us, he would have made contact by now." Seeing the sadness return to her face, he sighed, ashamed of himself. He hated upsetting her. "I'm sorry. I'll bring you some more flowers when I go back up."

She smiled. "The roses you brought me last time were lovely. It's too bad nothing colorful can grow down here."

That's why Xolotl always brought her something vibrant when he went to the surface. Sometimes he brought back colorful thread, or sweet and savory foods, or a beautifully-crafted instrument. But like everything in the underworld, those things soon lost their luster and joy, taking on the darker tones of death and depression. He wished Lady Death could come to the surface with him, just once, so she could see a world of more shades than just gray.

But as a death goddess, she was constrained to the

underworld; neither she nor her husband would ever know death the way mortals and the other gods did, but instead they were cursed to spend eternity in the shadows. Xolotl knew a great deal about death, but he'd never be a true death god, and so could walk among the living. A small blessing. But in trade he was forever bound to Lord Death, to serve as his master's window into the living world.

And he was Lady Death's eyes too. While Lord Death craved information about power struggles and deceptions, both mortal and divine, Xolotl reported to her on completely different things: life, love, and happiness. He was her only source for such things, and she drank up his rambling reports as if they were the finest blood. Lord Death rarely paid her mind, and when he did, it was usually with a glare or a grudging word.

I don't know why he keeps a wife at all, Xolotl thought. *Death gods are destroyers, and Lord Death has no physical desires, for he has no flesh. But Lady Death very much has flesh, and desire....*

His train of thought clouded and then he couldn't remember what he'd been thinking. *No matter,* he decided. "There are bright orange flowers that grow in the north, entire fields of them covering as far as the mortal eye can see. I'll bring you some and we can try planting them here. They are highly prolific and hardy, from what I've heard."

Lady Death patted his hand. "You're a truly good friend, Xolotl. I don't know what I'd do without you—"

But she suddenly fell silent, her eyes wide as she looked

past him.

Xolotl turned to see Lord Death standing in the doorway. Livid.

Lady Death scrambled to her feet, as did Xolotl, though much slower as he tried to balance himself against the wood slab table.

"A pleasure to see you again, My Lord." She bowed, sweeping her fingers across the ground at her feet.

But Lord Death spared her only a cursory glare before turning his loathing gaze on Xolotl.

Xolotl withered. He knew what to expect from such looks.

"Just when I think you can't possibly prove yourself any dumber, Xolotl," Lord Death snarled.

Xolotl looked from Lord Death to his wife then back again. "What did I do, My Lord?" His voice quaked.

"How many times have I reminded you to never go anywhere near the caverns when there are angels about?" Lord Death's voice shook the entire room; Lady Death steadied herself against the wall.

Xolotl gulped. "When you told me to leave and pointed here, I thought you wished me to check on your wife—"

"Why would I want you doing that with the Archangel himself watching? He asked where you were going!"

Lady Death paled.

Xolotl stuttered a moment before saying, "I'm sorry, My Lord, I didn't think—"

"You never think! You're an idiot! And I was an idiot to convince Michael to spare you from sitting on the Black Lake after the Conquest!" Lord Death struck Xolotl across the cheek with the back of his bony hand.

Xolotl shrieked as insects erupted from his pale, greenish flesh where Lord Death had touched him. When he fell over, Lord Death kicked him hard in the chest, causing another rupture. Xolotl writhed on the floor, beetles, spiders, and centipedes bursting from under his skin and crawling all over him.

Lady Death snatched up the clay jar and knelt next to him. "Be strong! It'll stop in a moment. Just hold on." She dusted the scurrying insects off of him into the jar.

When the last worm wriggled out, the torn flesh sealed up without blemish. Xolotl panted, tears flowing down his cheeks. *After millions of years of such punishment, one would think I'd be used to it by now.* He squeezed his one good eye shut.

Lady Death cast a scathing glare at her husband. Lord Death sneered and raised a hand as if to strike her too, but he stopped, an odd expression of hatred, frustration, and love crossing his skeletal face like shifting clouds. He turned away and leaned against the doorway, staring out into the ghost-lit hallway. "You have no consideration for her, Xolotl. Every time she finally settles somewhere, you force me to move her again."

Xolotl clamped his eye shut. He felt as if Lord Death had kicked him again, but this time it was guilt rather than insects scurrying out of his wounded flesh.

"Stop being so hard on him!" Lady Death snapped. "He's a good, loyal servant; he's not stupid or mean-spirited, which is more than I can say about you, My Lord."

"Don't lecture me on how I treat my servant," Lord Death growled. "He used to be reliable before you came along, with your worthless...pointless...scheming...." He gritted his teeth then shook his head. "I have enough trouble to deal with already without the added aggravation of having to relocate you yet again, so the angels don't find you."

"What trouble?" Lady Death asked.

"His most feathery grace informs me that he and his brothers are moving against the northern gods in the next several years, and they require the use of our 'useless space' to accommodate prisoners. Michael's even talking about moving those already subdued from the northeast here, the better for Raphael to keep a watchful eye on them. Mictlan will become a prison camp for all the remaining gods on this hemisphere."

Xolotl sat up, taken aback. "But many of them are our enemies!"

"Which means we'll have unwelcome company, including other death gods that hate us just as much as we do them. The angels are cramming us together, hoping our own conflicts will keep us out of their hair while they continue slicing up the spoils on earth, in the name of their father." Lord Death kicked over his wife's loom, punctuating his frustration.

"And what about the people?" Lady Death asked, worry painting her face. "Will they do to them as they did to our humans when the Spanish colonists came?"

"Who cares about the damn humans? The angels promised that Mictlan would remain intact, that I would retain control, but now we'll have less space to live, less places for you to hide."

It was on the tip of Xolotl's tongue to ask why they had to keep hiding her, but Lord Death turned to him. "This time, I won't tell you where I move her to. Then you can start thinking clearly again and get back to your rightful duties, to your rightful master."

Xolotl stared at him, confused and hurt, but when Lord Death advanced on him, he hurried to his feet again.

"Leave now, before I must kick you again," Lord Death snarled. "Go check on the gods and stay out of my sight while I figure out how to clean up after your stupidity."

Xolotl hobbled to the door. He stopped to glance back at Lady Death, who gave him a sympathetic smile, but Lord Death slashed the door curtain shut in his face. Sighing, he morphed back into a shaggy black wolf and headed away down the tunnel.

The despair and guilt eating at Xolotl eventually dissolved into simmering anger. "How many times did I stand up for him to the other gods, who all thought him stupid, who tried to trick or make a fool of him?" he rumbled under his breath as he cut across the plain towards the Black Lake. When he reached the banks, he plopped down on his rear and stared at the ground, tears winding down his snout and turning up puffs of dust when they landed at his feet. "Why do I even bother?"

Because you have to. You're sworn to serve him eternally,

and that includes defending him, even when he doesn't deserve it. The thought only made him grumpier though. "He's jealous that I can go topside while he's stuck down here in the dark forever. What if I decided to never come back? What would that old bag of bones do then?"

He'd probably be happy about it.

Xolotl's nape hairs bristled as he went to his feet, too wound up to sit still. "I bet he sat in the palace with those vultures, laughing while they all joke about how stupid I must be."

He soon found himself standing in front of Smoking Mirror. "None of them would be laughing if you were still around. And they wouldn't be talking about strapping us with even more gods. Michael would be dead and we wouldn't have to bow down to any angel's demands." He shook his head. "If only you were here now, Smoking Mirror...."

Xolotl sat contemplating this for a moment but then suddenly jumped to his feet as if struck by lightning. If Smoking Mirror were truly alive again, he'd make so much trouble that Michael wouldn't have time to move forward with the invasion of the north.

But Lord Death would never resurrect Smoking Mirror. He was too afraid of losing what little control of Mictlan he had now; Michael had him cowed and compliant. Besides, he never raised anyone without guaranteed compensation; he'd been burned too many times by sidestepped deals, and after the Quetzalcoatl/Mayahuel debacle—in which both of them robbed him of his promised rewards—he swore off deal-making all together.

He had a set price—half of all the power a given god accumulated from their sacrifices—and it had to be paid upfront and in full. No negotiation. He'd rather lick Michael's feet than be 'cheated' of his due.

But you know the words, remember? Lord Death never took care to keep his word magic secret from Xolotl; after all, he didn't believe his servant intelligent enough to know what to do with it. Nor did Xolotl have true death god magic....

Though when Xolotl consumed his master's insects, for a little while—a matter of an hour, sometimes less—a bit of death god magic coursed through him, allowing him to do things he normally couldn't. Like granting eternal rest to a restless spirit trapped on the plain because they gave their lives to a god that didn't have a heaven for their soul to ascend to. There weren't any more now, for Michael made Lord Death grant all trapped souls their final rest, but before the angels came, Lord Death never noticed one or two souls suddenly missing, for he'd kept an astonishingly large number of souls trapped there, just out of spite.

Xolotl had never tried to raise a god from the dead though. He'd eaten only a handful of the insects in Lady Death's home, and their magic would dissipate soon, so if he was going to try, it had to be now. He turned his eager gaze back up at Smoking Mirror.

The god sat slumped over, his long black hair tied in an intricate knot at the back of his head, with feathers and bones sticking out of it. His unblinking obsidian-mirror eyes reflected back the world in shades of grey, and behind those faintly-smiling lips were sharp, knife-like fangs that could send even the most stoic warrior into a terrified sprint. Xolotl had no history of hostilities with him, but he still wouldn't want to meet Smoking Mirror on a dark crossroads. *I'd love to see the look on Michael's face when he learns his arch nemesis has escaped prison,* Xolotl thought with a grin.

Collecting his thoughts, Xolotl leaned forward, closed his eye, and whispered,

"From dust to mud,
From mud to man,
Ignite his inner sun,
So he bleeds stars again."

He'd never actually spoken the words aloud—he'd heard Lord Death utter them a handful of times over the centuries—but now that he did, they sounded ridiculously simple to his ears. Silly, even.

And, unsurprisingly, nothing happened. Smoking Mirror's stare remained unchanged. Xolotl thought a moment then cursed himself under his breath; he needed to use the death magic, of course. Refocusing, he summoned the magic up inside himself, leaned forward again, and repeated the words, more forcefully this time.

But still nothing.

He tried a few more times, mustering all the magic he had to the surface so it tingled just under his skin as he spoke. But again, Smoking Mirror remained as dead as the previous three hundred years.

Xolotl hung his head. *Always the fool, thinking you can do such things. The master is right; you are a complete idiot.*

The smell of rain filled the air and Xolotl turned his nose towards the ceiling, puzzled. The mists hung thick, but no more than usual. A sudden *pop!*—like a stone dropped into water—echoed through the cavern, but when Xolotl turned around, the Black Lake's surface was mirror-smooth. But then a new smell joined in. "Flowers?"

When he looked down the line of gods along the lake's edge, a storm of flower petals swirled around the love goddess Xochiquetzal, casting a strange pink light around her. She sighed deeply then vanished with a *pop!*

Xolotl jumped to his feet. "Oh no! Oh no! Oh no!" He dashed to the next god in line—the hulking, half-feathered war god Mextli—then stood fidgeting as he tried to remember if he'd ever heard Lord Death utter a counter spell to make it stop. But the war god vanished too, like a column of brown and blue sand stripped away grain by grain by the wind. Everywhere he looked, the dead gods were disappearing in quick succession, turning into curious bubbles that floated away into the darkness above, or bursting into clouds of feathers. Panicked, Xolotl morphed into his human form and lunged at the nearest—Mextli's mother Coatlicue—but before he could close his arms around her, she vanished to the sound of rattlesnakes. He flew face-first into the reeds, raising a wooden clatter.

He brushed the dust from his face then sat up to look around. Only Smoking Mirror remained, still slouched, elbows on his knees. Xolotl let out a horrified gasp. The one he'd truly wanted to raise was the only one he didn't.

But now he smelled burning tobacco. Black smoke spilled out of Smoking Mirror's skin, slowly engulfing him. When it blew away, nothing remained.

Xolotl stared, stunned. For a moment he didn't know what to think or to feel, but then reality crashed down on him. "Omeyocan save me, what have I done?"

His master might forgive one god rising, but the whole lot...? Lord Death often told him there were things far worse than death, and now Xolotl dreaded he'd find out what those were.

You must run away and never come back! But that sent a stab of pain through him. As much as he daydreamed about leaving his cruel master, he never really could. He could leave the underworld for a few hundred years, but eventually he had to come back; the compulsion to obey his master overwhelmed everything. And even if he could withstand the urge, the pain would remind him of his bound servitude.

He stared around a moment, petrified, before he thought, *Go talk to Lady Death.* Yes, she'd know what to do. He morphed into a wolf and sprinted back to the cenote. Hopefully Lord Death hadn't moved her yet.

He dashed into the caves, but skidded to a halt when he came to a solid wall that hadn't been there before. He apparated to the other side to find himself standing in the middle of Lady Death's nearly empty one-room house; only she remained behind, knelt before the empty hearth, praying. Her own bright orange glow shed the only light in the darkness; a curious color for a death goddess's magic; his own was dull green, and Lord Death's was the palest blue...

But when his thoughts started clouding again, he shook the thought away. He had more important things on his mind. "Thank Omeyocan you're not gone yet!" he gasped, changing back to his gnarled human form and collapsing to his knees.

Lady Death came immediately to his side and put her arm around his shoulder. "What's the matter? Why are you shaking so?" The worry was thick in her voice. "What's happened?"

"I've done something so wrong...Lord Death is going to torture me until I beg for death, and he'll refuse to grant me that mercy!" he wailed.

"I doubt you could ever do anything that bad—"

"I raised all the gods from the dead!"

Her smile vanished and she blinked several times. "What do you mean?"

"I didn't think I could actually do it, and I was only trying to resurrect Smoking Mirror—"

"Why in Mictlan would you do that? Smoking Mirror tried to enslave the rest of us!"

The angry glint in her eyes made him cringe. "Yes, he did, but he's the only one who can defeat the angels; after all, he nearly killed Michael. And with the angels taking away everything they'd let us keep here in Mictlan...I thought he'd be a good sharp thorn in Michael's side," Xolotl said, his voice growing small as he realized just how foolish he sounded.

"But you raised all of them instead?"

"None are left at the Black Lake. What am I to do?" He gripped his head with both hands and rocked back and forth, a new terrifying thought hitting him. "Omeyocan save me, when Michael finds out what I did—"

"Why would Michael think you did it? He thinks you're a weak little fool who can't even use magic to scratch your own behind. He'll think Lord Death did this. And the bad news he delivered will just look like motivation."

"Oh no! The master—" Xolotl covered his head with his arms.

"What's the worse they could do to him? It's not as if Michael can kill him."

"No, but we'll lose Mictlan forever! And Michael just might consider the rest of us too much of a hassle to keep around, even dead. He already wanted to throw Smoking Mirror into the Black Lake.... Oh, why didn't I think this through before uttering those cursed words?"

Sharing his growing panic, Lady Death took to pacing the tiny room. "Lord Death must know what's happened, but it would be best if we went to him with a plan for fixing it."

"There is no way to fix this," Xolotl wept.

"You could bring them back to the lakeside, and if you do it quickly enough, Michael won't know anything. The angels only inspect Mictlan once a year, and Michael doesn't intend to move on the north for several more years yet, so we have time."

"But that's over fifty gods...and when they regain their memories, they won't come back willingly. It's no easy thing to kill a god who knows he's one."

"Then get them before they regain their memories—"

"But they have to regain their memories, or they go into oblivion when they die," Xolotl reminded her.

Lady Death frowned. "Oh yes, that's right."

And to think she's a death goddess. But again his mind fogged. He shook it off, annoyed.

"You needn't kill them though," she went on. "The living can walk the road into Mictlan, so if you can get to them quickly and convince them to walk the road with you, then Lord Death can deal with them once they get here."

It was as good a plan as any, but Xolotl still hesitated. "Must we truly tell the master what I've done?"

"He needs to know, so he can do his part." Lady Death gave him a sweet, reassuring smile. "But don't worry; I won't let him anywhere near you."

Lady Death and Xolotl apparated directly into the obsidian and bone palace, something Lord Death forbade her from ever doing, but once Xolotl laid out the situation, he forgot his anger at his wife and instead sat very still upon his throne of jade bones, focusing his loathing stare at his servant. Usually he sat to one side, because of the throne's missing arm—he'd lost the large femur to the wind god long ago, in a game that remained a contentious subject for him—but instead he sat straight upright, his balled fists on his lap, his ghost light eyes burning brighter than ever. Even when Xolotl finished, he still didn't say anything. But he ground his teeth so loud that the throne room's obsidian walls vibrated.

Xolotl finally dared venture his gaze up to meet his master's face, confused as to why Lord Death hadn't yet spoken. That's when his master launched from his chair, reaching out to throttle him.

But Lady Death herself jumped between them, and Lord Death recoiled. Pain, disgust, and fear painted his face, as if her very proximity troubled him. "You protect him now, but when Michael finds out...none of us will be safe!" he protested, petulant. "And when he finds you here—"

"Xolotl will bring them back, and you will return them to the banks of the Black Lake." She stepped closer, making him retreat back to his throne. "He'll work as quickly as he can, so they're here before the next inspection."

"Even if he weren't a complete incompetent, he could never return all of them before Raphael's next visit."

"It won't be an easy task," Lady Death admitted. "But if he had help—"

"Don't even suggest it," Lord Death snapped.

"You can't leave the underworld to help him—"

"And neither can you." Lord Death loomed over her, all fear forgotten. "It's not open for discussion."

Lady Death didn't wither but she fell silent. He glared at her before turning his back to them and going to the window of obsidian glass behind his throne, overlooking the Black Lake. "If a good number of the missing gods are returned to the lakeside by the time Raphael comes for his next inspection, perhaps he might be convinced that we're repentant and trying to correct a very unfortunate accident. Angels like that kind of thing."

"And you have said that Raphael is rather reasonable compared to other angels," Lady Death said.

Xolotl nodded, daring to hope this wasn't a completely fatal blunder. "And Michael tried to throw Smoking Mirror into the Black Lake today, but Raphael stopped him."

Lord Death cocked his head, thoughtful. After a moment, he turned to Xolotl again. "Don't bother coming back until you have at least one god in your possession."

"Yes, My Lord." Xolotl bowed low.

"And if Michael finds out, I won't come to your rescue or beg him to spare you. You own all of this, and I wash my hands of you." He turned away again, looking strangely exhausted. "Now get out of my sight."

Xolotl morphed into a wolf and trotted from the throne room, desperate to get away before his master decided a parting kick was in order.

When he reached the towering doors leading outside, Lady Death called for him to wait. Kneeling in front of him, she took his face between her hands. "Promise you'll see me again really soon, my friend."

A pang of fear stabbed his guts. "You really think I can do this?"

"I have absolute faith in you." She kissed him between the eyes. "You should have more faith in yourself."

A sensation like a warm blanket curled around him, fortifying him. "I will see you again soon, My Lady, and I'll bring you something beautiful when I do."

She laughed. "Seeing you again will be gift enough."

Xolotl half expected to find angels waiting for him outside the palace doors, swords drawn to smite him into oblivion, but to his relief, when he nudged the massive doors of bone open, only the dry plain of Mictlan sat before him. He wasted no time though; as soon as he crossed the threshold into the courtyard, he apparated out of the underworld. Most gods couldn't apparate out of Mictlan; that power rested with Lord Death, who, ironically, couldn't use the power for himself. Xolotl could sometimes do it himself too, thanks to his steady diet of his master's magical insects.

The sun shone hot and bright in the afternoon sky when Xolotl appeared in a hayfield, startling a nesting quail into flight. He attuned his divine senses, to help him decide where to start searching for the others, but he felt nothing but angelic magic radiating down from Omeyocan above. The world was no different than it had been for the last three hundred years.

No, it is slightly different. He closed his good eye and

concentrated. Sometimes it was impossible to hear anything past the static muttering of prayers, particularly since today was what the angels called the Sabbath, so the interference was particularly loud. But something else—something new—whispered among the prayers.

Xolotl disappeared with a snap then rematerialized on the edge of a cornfield, hot wind swaying the tall green stalks. A canal gurgled behind him, running the length of the field, fenced on the far side by hedges of Osage Orange trees. Their thick mat of spiny branches obliterated any view of what lay beyond. A ground squirrel chattered at him before disappearing among the branches. In the distance a cow lowed.

Xolotl extended his divine senses again, but the whispering vanished. The sounds of prayers were quieter here but still ever-present—prayers for a dying loved one, prayers for good health, prayers for the strength to deal with difficult times. These were different than the prayers humans used to say before the angels came. Back then, people begged for rain so the maize wouldn't die, or they implored the war god to punish their enemies, or they asked the god of the hunt to bless their drawn bow as they sighted a deer. As Xolotl opened his eye again, the prayers faded away, leaving only the wind rustling through the hedge.

A winged shadow crossing the ground in front of him sent him darting into the thorny hedge, but when he looked up, he spotted a low-flying hawk scanning for a meal. He exhaled sharply. *You haven't time for this nonsense.* He crawled out, cringing as the cuts and scrapes healed themselves.

He followed the canal to its end then wound through the field, searching with his fully-open senses. Despite the annoying background noise, the whisper remained frustratingly silent. He eventually emerged from the corn rows into the dirt yard of a plank-board house. Already the sun was creeping down below the horizon.

Someone must be here. A shiver of divine power vibrated in the ground, completely unlike that now-familiar angelic magic. It was very old, from before the Fifth Sun rose for the first time, so it could only be one of a handful of gods—

"Mama! Look! A dog!"

Xolotl started at seeing a girl in a patchwork dress sitting on the house's slanted front steps. A woman unclipped laundry from the line stretching from the porch to the lamp post in the yard.

But when the woman looked up and saw Xolotl, she swooped for the porch, leaving a shirt dangling by one clothespin. She grabbed a broom and held it out like a spear, jabbing at him. "Get out of here!" She nudged the girl up the steps, towards the door. "Rory! Get the rifle! There's a bloody wolf out here!"

Xolotl dashed back into the cornfield; he knew all too well about rifles. Most humans were afraid of his wolf-like form, but the Europeans weren't afraid to turn their weapons on him. Apparently wolves were vicious, man-eating monsters back in Europe. He'd been shot a couple of times in the early colonial years, but he quickly figured out that a more dog-like appearance helped. The Spanish loved their war hounds—murderous as those beasts were—and the closer he resembled them, the better they treated him. He continued changing it over the years as he came into increasing contact with Americans, who were fond of lean, floppy-eared hounds; among them he favored a foxhound: tri-colored and sweet in temperament, and he never failed to get a smile and a pat. He maintained the wolf-form for his master, who disapproved of any softening of his appearance, but in his haste to get to work tracking down the other gods, he'd forgotten to change.

Idiot! he scolded himself as he morphed into a hound then lay among the stalks, listening. Someone moved through the field, but far enough away to pose little risk. The shadows grew darker with sunset and soon it was too difficult to see anything.

"Get back here, Rory," the woman called. "I don't want you in that field when it gets dark. Let your father deal with it."

"It's probably taken off by now," a boy called back, from closer than Xolotl liked. He couldn't see him in the twilight, but he heard him rattling the stalks as he walked back to the house. "When's Da coming back?"

"He said before dark," the woman answered, worry in her voice. "There's never just one wolf around, and I still have laundry to pack in."

"I'll stand guard while you finish, Mama."

"Fiona, go inside and check on the soup."

"But the soup's just fine," the girl whined. "I checked on it not ten minutes ago."

"Do what Mama tells you!" Rory snarled. "I have enough to watch out here without you hobbling—"

"Rory!" his mother snapped. "Mind your tongue!"

"I didn't mean anything by it, Mama—"

"The Good Lord makes us all special; it's just more obvious to the eyes for some folks."

After a tense silence, Rory said, "I'm sorry, Fiona."

"Now get inside and check on that soup, and no more lip, young lady." the mother said. This time the door slammed shut and no one said anything, letting the clothesline twang softly as someone plucked off the pins one after another. Xolotl remained still until footsteps echoed on the wooden stairs and the door slammed again. By then darkness had fallen.

He moved towards the house again, keeping to the shadows. He still felt the faint vibrations of divine energy, but before long, the clomping of horse hooves drove him back into the field. At this rate, he'd never find the source of the energy.

A man on horseback cantered into the yard, and the woman came out again, bringing an oil lamp. "I was starting to worry for you, Collin. Supper's on the table."

"Thunder threw a shoe, so I had to get him reshod before coming home." Collin dismounted. "I'll be in as soon as I put him to bed."

"Be careful. There was a wolf out by the field this evening."

Collin stared into the corn and Xolotl pressed his body to the ground. "You'd best head inside then. I'll be right in." Taking the oil lamp, he led the horse around the side of the house.

The woman brought out a second lamp and hung it from the nail next to the door. She cast a fretful stare out into the cornstalks before disappearing inside. The man looked again too when he came back a few moments later, the saddle over his shoulder and a shotgun tucked under his arm.

Once the front door slammed, Xolotl hurried to the dark side of the house. He kept close to the stone foundation, to remain unseen from the windows, and followed his senses around to the back.

The vibrations came from everywhere, and the moonless night made it difficult to see much. *Maybe they're all here.* That would make matters easier; he'd just have to convince them all to come with him.

Rustling in the cornfield made him freeze. Bitter sulfur suffused the air, and the horse whinnied in the barn while the goats took to bleating and stomping around their pen nearby. A pulse of fear bit into him when he looked to the sky to see that not only was the sky moonless, but the stars were gone too. *Michael lets the Tzitzimime wander free?* The cornstalks rattled again, and Xolotl jumped when red eyes burned in the dark between the rows. *The stars have come down to earth!* As he started backing away, guttural growls rose like a chorus of singing cicada, and more eyes joined the first set.

"Go back to where you came from!" Xolotl tried for forceful but his voice cracked. "You've no business here, star demons!"

"You aren't our mistress," a voice growled from the

dark. "We obey our Lady of the Golden Bells, not some weak godling sworn to lick Death's feet." Several spiny, dog-like shadows stepped from the cornfield. "We've sensed our mistress's return, so we prepare for her arrival."

The goats began stampeding around their pen. Xolotl turned to see three star demons slinking over the fence, their grotesque, hairless bodies clearly visible in the lamplight from the barn door. They flexed the thick quills on their necks and leaped upon the goats, grabbing them by the necks with their needle-like fangs. The goats bleated, eyes wide and terrified as the star demons swarmed the pen.

Two star demons remained by the corn, watching Xolotl. "Animal blood fills," one growled, "but god's blood is even better." They advanced on him.

Xolotl backed up, startled. "You threaten me? I'm Lord Death's messenger!"

They laughed. "We'd best send you back to your master, before he fears you've wandered off." They sprang.

Xolotl turned to run but the star demons fell upon him, growling and snapping. They bit his neck and shoulders, sucking his magic out of him in brutally long pulls that made his skin feel as if it were shrinking in upon itself. Turning human—the better to grip onto them—he tore them off one after the other, but when he apparated away, he suddenly rematerialized on the other side of the house, at the foot of the steps. He collapsed into the dirt, his magic gushing out in spurts of gold dust from his wounds. He healed himself and changed back into a dog, but when he tried to apparate again, nothing happened. He'd used up all of his magic. The star demons skittered around the corner, and he made to run but fell over, too weak to keep to his feet.

The house's front door banged and the star demons looked up. A deafening blast took off half of the head of the closest one. The second one yelped, his shoulder and face pock-marked with buckshot. He dashed off into the dark while the other one swayed on its feet before collapsing with a mangled cry.

Collin held his shotgun with both hands, his eyes wide with disbelief. "What in Heaven's name...."

Rory rushed out, rifle in hand. He too gaped at the dead star demon.

But the horse's terrified cries broke the spell, and Collin leaped off the porch, reloading his shotgun as he ran for the barn. "Give Rory the extra ammunition, Alanna!" He disappeared around the corner and more gunfire rang out, followed by shrieks and howls. Rory rushed back inside, shoving his mother and sister aside in his hurry.

The girl—Fiona—peered around her mother shoulder. "What's going on?" She glared at Rory when he pushed her aside on his way back outside. But when he jumped off the porch, she spotted Xolotl lying at the bottom of the stairs. "What's that?" She pointed.

Alanna pulled back. "I think it's the wolf!"

Fiona stepped past her mother for a closer look. "No, look! It's just a dog." When Xolotl renewed his efforts to get up, but fell over again, she hurried for the steps. "He's hurt!"

But her mother grabbed her arm. "He could be sick, Fiona! Let your father deal with him."

More gunfire rang through the night, followed by Rory yelling, "We've got them on the run now, Da! That'll teach them to come skulking around our farm!"

Xolotl again struggled to get to his feet but his legs refused to hold him.

"He needs help, Mama!" Fiona tried to pry her mother's fingers from her arm, but the woman held tight.

Collin finally came back, pausing to poke at the star demon with his shotgun. "Good Lord Almighty, what on earth is this thing?"

"You've never seen anything like it, Da?" Rory asked over his shoulder.

He scratched his chin. "It could be a coyote with bad mange, but what are those things sticking out like that?" He prodded the quills at the star demon's nape.

"It's probably that wolf we saw earlier," Alanna said.

"That isn't any wolf," Collin muttered.

"There's a bunch of them over by the barn," Rory said. "You don't want to see what they did to your goats, Mama."

When Alanna shot a questioning look at her husband, he nodded. "We lost every last one, and these things nearly got at Thunder. Rory and me will keep a watch tonight, make sure they don't come back, and I'll fix the barn door in the morning."

He then turned his gaze to Xolotl struggling mightily to get up. He went over and prodded Xolotl's ribs with the barrel of his shotgun.

Xolotl rolled over on his back, ears flat to his head and front paws curled in submission. He'd learned such tricks from watching real dogs. The gun couldn't kill him, but it still smarted to be shot.

"He's hurt, Da," Fiona said. "Can't we do anything for him?"

Collin knelt to give Xolotl's chest a gentle pat. "I don't see any wounds on him, but the light is poor out here."

"We should bring him inside." When her mother began protesting, Fiona added, "We can't leave him out here, Mama. What if those coyotes come back?"

Indeed, it could be hours before moonrise and Xolotl was too weak to defend himself against another attack. At least inside he might find something to rejuvenate his magic, an absolute necessity before making any attempt to confront one of the newly-risen gods.

"And what if he bites one of you children?" Alanna fired back.

"He's not going to bite anyone." Collin smiled when Xolotl thumped his tail reassuringly. "He seems a good boy. I'm sure he belongs to someone and they'll appreciate us taking him in for the night." He handed the shotgun off to Rory then scooped Xolotl into his arms.

"You keep him out of my kitchen!" Alanna warned as her husband walked by her into the house.

Collin set Xolotl on a threadbare rug in front of the fireplace then sat next to him. He felt for his bones and joints—and Xolotl's magic provided evidence of them as needed—and pushed gently on his soft belly. "Well, I don't see anything wrong with him, aside from that eye, but that looks like an old wound. He's probably just exhausted. A good night's rest and he'll be right by morning."

"Then let's get back to the table, before the food goes completely cold," Alanna ordered.

Rory dove back into his food, but Fiona lingered crouched next to Xolotl, rubbing one of his floppy ear between her fingers.

"Let him sleep, dear," her father said with a gentle smile, and she finally returned to her chair. When she glanced back at Xolotl and smiled at him over her shoulder, he turned his back to her and kept his eye closed, pretending to sleep.

He opened his eye again though when the front door slammed a little while later. He looked up to find himself alone at last; Alanna hummed in the kitchen, out of sight beyond the doorway to the left of the table, and one of the two bedroom doors was closed. He listened for the others before crawling along on his belly, seeking out whatever beetles and spiders he could find. But there were few—and none as filling as Lord Death's insects—so he soon returned to the rug, no stronger than before. *I need blood.*

All gods needed blood; even angels did, though that was a well-guarded secret. He had to be cautious in getting it though. Human blood was most potent, but feeding on humans was a capital offense under the angels' rule. Nor was it smart to bite one of the children; he had no doubt Collin wouldn't hesitate to shoot him at the first sign of danger.

Soon Collin and Rory came back, the father carrying two skinned and disemboweled goats, and his son toting a tin pail full of sloshing liquid. Xolotl eyed the pail, smelling blood, and when they went into the kitchen, he scooted after, lapping up after Rory's slopping. *Not very warm but good enough.* Already his magic began rebuilding. When Rory set the pail down, Xolotl stuck his head in and started lapping greedily.

"Jesus, Mary, and Joseph!" Alanna cried. "I was going to make black pudding with that!" She picked up her broom to shoo him away but he ignored her, drinking it up even faster. "Collin! He's ruining it!"

Rory wrapped his arms around Xolotl's midsection and pulled him away, but Xolotl clawed at the floor with his front paws, fighting to get back to the bucket.

Collin laughed. "Looks like he's hungry."

"For Heaven's sake, get him out of here, Rory!" Alana shouted. "Put him outside!"

"But what if the wolves come back?" Rory panted, half laughing under his labored breath as Xolotl wiggled in his arms.

Collin headed for the storeroom with the carcasses. "Just let him finish it already. It'll just go to waste otherwise."

Alanna sighed but nodded, so Rory let Xolotl go. Xolotl rushed back to the bucket.

"It wouldn't have kept until morning anyway," Collin said.

"I know. It's just...it's frustrating, losing so many animals all at once. Such a waste! We're having a hard enough time as it is—"

"We can sell most of the meat in town, and as for the rest, we'll salt it and save it for winter." He kissed her cheek. "We'll be just fine. I'll fix the barn and fortify the chicken coop, and there are plenty of rabbits to hunt around here." He glanced again at Xolotl, thoughtful. "We could use a good hunting dog, you know."

Alanna pinned him with a chastising glare. "You need to take him to town tomorrow, to see if he belongs to anyone."

"I will, but if no one claims him, I see no reason we couldn't keep him."

Rory smiled, excited.

"And if someone does claim him?" she went on.

Collin shrugged. "We'll buy one of our own."

"With what money? We haven't any. And you better not think about keeping him secret. That's no Christian thing to do, Collin Molloy."

He frowned at her. "I never said anything about stealing him. I *will* take him to town tomorrow." He grabbed up his shotgun from the butcher block. To Rory, he barked, "And off to bed with you. Your watch is in a few hours." The front door slammed as he went outside.

Once Rory retreated from the kitchen, Xolotl looked from the bucket to Alanna, his magic finally glutted. She frowned at him, so he wagged his tail in thanks. She sighed then patted her leg gently with her hand.

He knew what the gesture meant, but he didn't like humans touching him unless absolutely necessary. However, they did expect friendly dogs to want pats on the head or scratches on the ribs, so he finally padded over and let her rub his ears with both hands as she knelt in front of him.

"You are a handsome devil, even with that unfortunate eye. Maybe this time we'll get lucky and you'll be looking for a home."

I'll be gone in the morning, he thought but merely wagged his tail. It was a capital crime for his kind to speak to humans when not in a human form.

"At the very least Fiona could use someone to watch over her while I'm working, and she seems sweet on you. Maybe...." But Alanna shook her head. "No, I'm not going to get my hopes up. I thought things would be better for coming out here, but it's been one disappointment after another. Though I guess we're luckier than most; we got out before the potato famine hit real hard, and Collin didn't have to take a railroad job. I just wish the school would let Fiona in; she's smart as any boy, but they say any vacant chair should go to someone with a future. As if my little girl has no future—" She choked on her words, and went on again once she'd bit back tears. "But if you ask me, it's because we're Catholic." She sighed. "We should have stayed in Boston."

Xolotl pretended to listen, but he couldn't have cared less. Considering his own troubles, human problems were so quaint.

Alanna smiled again and patted his head. "Yes, a handsome devil indeed." She left for bed.

Xolotl returned to the rug in front of the fireplace. He'd

sneak out once the moon had risen, but for now, he rested his head on his paws, closed his eye, and opened his divine senses again, searching for that vibration that had brought him here to start with.

But all he felt now was the sinister thrum of star demon magic.

But the moon didn't rise until nearly dawn, and the star demons prowled all night, their cries and howls a constant reminder that it wasn't safe to venture out. There was no gunfire, so they were staying away from the farm, but Xolotl decided it was best to wait until morning, when the rising sun would drive the demons back into hiding.

Rory relieved his father's watch before sunrise, but Collin only slept a few hours before rising to do chores. Alanna woke shortly after her husband and set about stoking the kitchen fire for breakfast. Soon the smell of hot cornbread drew Rory inside and Fiona out of bed. Xolotl maintained his fake slumber in front of the fireplace.

But he started awake when Fiona gave him a clumsy hug around the neck. "Good morning, Travis." And even worse, she kissed his forehead.

He stared back at her, too disconcerted to think of how he should react.

"Travis?" Rory asked. "What are you calling him that for?"

Fiona rubbed the kissed spot with her hand. "Because

Mama always said that William Travis was a handsome devil, and she says the same thing about him." She inclined her head towards Xolotl. "And she's right; he's one good-looking dog. Such lovely markings; those brown patches over his eyes look like big, bushy eyebrows."

"Yeah well, it's a dumb name for a dog." Rory bit into his cornbread.

"It's not dumb. It suits him just fine. Doesn't it, Mama?"

"What suits him?" Alanna set a jug of syrup on the table and when Rory reached for it, she slapped his hand. "Not before your father gets his."

"I named the dog William Travis," Fiona said.

"You shouldn't name him, Fiona. You'll be right upset when your father finds his master and gives him back."

Fiona shook her head. "No, he's going be with us a good long time. I can feel it."

Collin came in with a length of rope over his shoulder, and he too grabbed a piece of cornbread. Alanna poured syrup on it for him. "You've got the goat wrapped and packed?" she asked.

He nodded, waiting to swallow before asking, "Would you please salt the rest while I'm gone? It needs done before the flies start swarming."

"I will." She kissed his cheek.

"And you're to muck all that stuff out of the goat pen by the time I get back," he told Rory. "Give it to the pigs." He then looped the rope around Xolotl's neck.

What in Mictlan! Xolotl pulled away, but the rope drew tight. *Apparate! Apparate!* he thought, but his better sense won out in time. He thrashed back and forth, trying to bite the rope.

"He doesn't like that, Da!" Fiona protested.

"He'll be fine."

"Must you really take him with you? Can't he stay here, until you know who he belongs to?"

Collin smiled and rubbed her cheek with his callused hand. "If things don't work out, we'll get a puppy for Christmas."

Alanna glared at him. Fiona sighed fretfully as her father pulled Xolotl out the front door.

Xolotl continued thrashing, and tripped down the stairs. When he tumbled around, trying to regain his feet, Collin picked him up and set him upright in the back of the wagon. He tied the rope to the seat, so Xolotl couldn't jump out. He finished by ruffling Xolotl's ears.

Maybe I'll bite you anyway. Xolotl glared at his back as Collin climbed up onto the wooden bench.

Looking forlorn, Fiona waved goodbye from the porch as they rambled off down the road.

And now the man took to singing old Irish song off-key and so loud it even drown out the clack of the horse's hooves and the creak of the wheels. Xolotl growled, but he remained focused on the road behind them, waiting for the house to disappear from sight. Once they turned the corner down the lane, Xolotl finally apparated away, relieved to be free of the rope and Collin's terrible howling.

He rematerialized in the middle of the cornfield, and trotted back towards the house, but once he reached the backyard, he hunkered down among the rows.

Rory stood barefoot in the fly-infested goat pen, his pant legs rolled up to his knees as he mucked out the remains of the goats with a shovel. Fiona sat at the top step of the back porch, holding a bandelure by its string, watching the wooden wheel spin, disappointment on her face. Good. They were both distracted.

Keeping close to the ground, Xolotl scurried to the shaded side of the house, out of their view. He raised his nose to the wind and opened his divine senses, scanning for the whisper again.

"Why don't you make yourself useful and go get me a cup of water," Rory said.

"Go get it yourself," Fiona replied.

"Just because you're a dumb cripple doesn't mean you get to sit there on your arse all the time."

Xolotl blinked, taken aback. His mission suddenly forgotten, he hurried to the corner of the house and peered around the edge.

Fiona yanked the string off her finger and threw the bandelure at Rory, pegging him in the back. "Why are you always as mean as a two-legged cur, Rory?" She clambered down the stairs, across the yard to the pen.

Xolotl gaped: her left leg was shorter than the other, giving her a strange, ungainly walk that he knew all too well. *She's like me!* He'd never seen a deformed child before; such infants had always been given to the priests for a sacrifice; most human parents couldn't afford such a burden, and the rain god Tlaloc preferred the blood of young children. The souls of sacrifices went directly to the heaven of the god they honored, so Xolotl had never had occasion to meet one.

Rory laid into Fiona some more about her gimp leg, but Xolotl heard Lord Death's voice instead, going over and over in his head: *It must tire you so, being not only physically deformed, but mentally as well....*

"Stop it!" Xolotl shouted at the boy.

Both children looked over, startled. But then Fiona's face lit with joy. "Travis! You've come back!" She ambled over and put her arms around his neck.

Xolotl glared at Rory past Fiona's shoulder. *I must accept such abuse without complaint, but I won't stand by and let* you *kick her around.*

His own thoughts startled him; since when did he care about humans anymore? True, he used to guide their dead, but their offerings to him had long dried up, leaving him wholly reliant on his master for magic. And yet he felt strangely protective of this girl.

"Who said that?" Rory climbed the fence, muck clinging to his bare feet. "Who's over there?" he called towards the cornfield.

Alanna nudged the backdoor open with her elbow, her hands covered in salt paste. "What's going on out here?"

Rory dashed into the house. "Someone's hiding in the cornfield."

"My floor! Look at the mess you're making!"

"I'll clean it up, Mama," he called from further inside.

When Alanna noticed Xolotl standing next to Fiona, she leaned forward, to peer towards the road. "Your father's back already?"

"I don't think so." Fiona stroked Xolotl's head. "Travis came back, so it must be a sign, Mama."

"A sign he got off his rope," Alanna muttered.

Rory jumped out the back door, shotgun in hand.

"You be careful with that thing!"

"I will, Mama." He headed for the cornfield.

Alanna motioned to her daughter but kept her gaze fixed on her son. "You should come inside, Fiona."

"It's probably just those horrible Harrison boys, snuck away from their chores to spy on us," Fiona said. "Rory will make them pull foot."

Rory poked around the cornstalks with his gun. "Come out and show yourself!" When no one answered, he added, "If I have to come in there after you, you'll get an arse full of buckshot!"

"Rory!" his mother hollered. "Watch your language!"

He turned to Xolotl. "Let's get the dog to flush them out." He patted his leg. "Come here, boy!"

Xolotl glared back at him and rumbled in his throat. *You're not my master, human.*

Rory called to him a couple more times before giving up. "That dog's dumb as a stump."

"He's not stupid!" Fiona fired back.

Rory laughed. "Rich. One mush-head defending another."

Xolotl hadn't noticed Alanna leave the porch until she smacked Rory upside the head. The boy yowled and rubbed the back of his skull with his free hand. "That's worth three strokes with the belt when your father returns. Now get back to mucking out that pen, because if it isn't done, it'll be six instead of three."

Rory rubbed the back of his head, consternation on his face. "Sorry, Mama."

"And you come help me with the salt," she told Fiona. "And no arguing. Go open the door for me."

Fiona sighed but obeyed.

Once they were alone in the yard, Rory turned to sneer at Xolotl. Xolotl returned the gesture.

"What are you curling your lip at me for, you mangy mongrel?" Rory kicked muck at him.

Xolotl didn't back down but once Rory turned his back to him, he slunk off into the cornfield.

"Now you go, you dumb mutt," Rory called after him. "I hope a wolf eats you!"

Xolotl growled in his throat. *If you knew who I really was, you'd watch your tongue.*

But now wasn't the time for distraction. He focused his senses again, trying to put Rory and Fiona out of his mind. Almost immediately, he felt the ground vibrating with magic. He followed the tingling to the canal where he'd first arrived yesterday.

The water ran lower now, and an eerie hush blanketed the sticky, humid air, as if every living thing were holding its breath.

Then he heard slurping, and the water in the canal lowered still more.

When he looked towards the large cottonwood growing out of the crumbled bank, he spotted a creature—only vaguely human-looking—hanging over the side of the canal. It sucked in great mouthfuls of water, its body expanding like a bloated toad with each intake, but it returned to normal size again as soon as it stopped. The creature panted, staring into the water before dipping in again. Stone goggles embedded in the flesh of its face obscured its eyes.

Tlaloc. Xolotl breathed a relieved sigh and trotted down the bank towards him.

Tlaloc started as he approached, and backed away from the water, but he remained crouched next to the tree.

"I'm not going to hurt you," Xolotl called from the opposite bank. "Do you know who I am?"

Tlaloc squinted at him through his goggles half-filled with water. "I can't see well. My eyes hurt."

"Slosh them with water," Xolotl suggested.

The rain god eyed him before tossing his head around. A smile hinted at his lips. "That *is* better." He gazed back at Xolotl, contemplative. "Who are you?"

"I'm like you. You can feel my magic, can't you?"

Raising his nose to the air, Tlaloc sniffed. "Yours doesn't smell like mine." He eyed him suspiciously.

"Do you know who you are?"

Tlaloc cast his gaze down the canal, avoiding eye contact. "I don't remember."

Good.

"Do *you* know who I am?" he asked.

"My master knows, and he can help you regain your memory."

Tlaloc glowered a moment then looked down at the water again. "I'm so thirsty, but no matter how much I drink, I just feel thirstier."

"My master can help with that too."

"Where is he?" Tlaloc sniffed the air.

"I'll take you to him right now. We can be there in a few moments—"

But a gasp from the cornstalks cut him off. Xolotl turned to see Fiona staring at him with wide, amazed eyes. "You can talk!" she cried.

Tlaloc came to his feet for a better look. He licked his lips, anxious.

Xolotl nudged Fiona back into the rows. *You can't be here! It's a very, very bad thing!* While Tlaloc's memory was gone, his divine appetites worked on instinct, and after three hundred years of not feeding, the hunger would be insistent.

"Have you always been able to talk?" she asked.

This mission had become one disaster after another, but perhaps if he acted very dog-like, she would think she'd only imagined hearing him talking. He nudged her again, and barked and whined, hoping he sounded distressed enough to make her reconsider.

She stumbled backwards but chattered on. "You yelled at Rory back there, didn't you? How did you learn to talk?" She pushed his nose aside and refused to budge anymore when he tried again to nudge her on. "I know you can talk, so why don't you say something?"

"You must get out of here, now!" Xolotl finally hissed, exasperated. "It's not safe!"

She smiled wide, vindicated. "I knew I hadn't imagined it. Rory!" she yelled, looking back towards the house. "Rory! Come right away! You won't believe this!"

"No! Don't call him over here! It's dangerous!" He chanced a glance back at Tlaloc, who was now sniffing the air with interest.

"Back here by the canal, Rory!" she called again.

Xolotl grabbed hold of her dress hem with his teeth and started dragging her towards the house.

But within a few steps, she went over face-first into the damp dirt. She blinked, startled. "What did you do that for?"

Without answering, he dashed back to the canal. *I'll have to risk her seeing me apparate away with Tlaloc.*

But when he reached the water, Tlaloc was gone. He looked up and down the canal. "Oh for Mictlan's sake!" He closed his good eye and focused his divine senses. He still felt Tlaloc nearby....

Rory burst out of the cornrows, panting and looking around with wide, worried eyes. When he spotted Fiona dusting dirt off of her dress, he rushed to her. "Are you all right?"

"Of course I'm fine, but this is really exciting, Rory!" Fiona pointed at Xolotl. "He can talk!"

Rory stared at Xolotl but then glared at Fiona. "I thought you were in trouble, but instead you're on about dumb talking dogs?"

"He really can!" She turned to Xolotl. "Go ahead, Travis, say something to Rory."

But before Xolotl could do anything, Rory shouted, "Don't ever do that again!" He punched her in the shoulder, knocking her over backward. He inhaled sharply and recoiled. "I'm sorry, Fiona, I didn't mean—"

Death's Good Dog

He started helping her back up.

But when Xolotl saw the first of several tears leaking down Fiona's cheeks, he gasped. "You must stop crying!"

Rory stared at him, his jaw hanging open.

"If he smells your tears—"

But something knocked him aside.

Fiona screamed.

Tlaloc lunged at her, but Rory threw himself between them. "No!"

Tlaloc snatched him in both arms then dragged him back to the canal, his tiny eyes squinting blindly, his lips curled up in an eager growl. They disappeared over the edge with a splash, Rory still struggling.

Fiona screamed louder, her tears flowing faster now.

"Get out of here! Go! Now!" Xolotl hurried to the edge of the canal. Below, Rory thrashed his arms and legs wildly while Tlaloc held his head under the water. Xolotl leaped off the bank and tried to tackle the rain god, but Tlaloc decked him aside and snarled like an animal protecting its kill.

Xolotl dragged himself back ashore, stunned at having been so easily knocked aside. *If he kills the boy—*

But then Rory stopped struggling. An ecstatic expression spread over Tlaloc's face and water completely filled his goggles. "Yes!" His roar came like thunder and shook the ground. "More!"

Xolotl rushed back to Fiona, who sat staring in terror. He nipped at her legs to bring her back. "Get out of here, now! No waiting!"

She finally lumbered to her feet, stumbling and falling

over at first, but then she ran as fast as her shortened leg would permit, screaming for her mother.

Tlaloc rose from the canal on a geyser of water. "You dare run off my sacrifice?" He pelted Xolotl with water, sprawling him against the cornstalks. He bared his tusk-like fangs. "Take me to your master, will you? I remember you, Black Dog; a coward and a sneak, and your master is a pitiless fool who'd rather rule over his brothers than help them! You dare try to send me back to the Black Lake, you treacherous, lying gimp?" He blasted more water at Xolotl, sending him tumbling through the cornrows. "Bring me the girl or I'll send you back to your master the same way Michael sent me to Mictlan!"

Xolotl finally found his feet and dashed for the farm house. *Now you've done it. No way Michael won't find out!*

When he came out into the yard, Fiona was clutching her mother, not saying anything, just panting, eyes wild. Alanna yelled at her to say something—anything—her own growing panic getting the better of her.

She was so loud that she didn't notice Collin until he pulled the wagon into the yard. He jumped down and ran to her. "What's going on? Is she all right?"

"I don't know!" Alanna cried. "She was screaming, but now...I think she's in shock."

Collin pulled Fiona into his arms. "It's all right, darling, you're safe now. Just tell your Da what's the matter."

But Fiona only blinked at him with no understanding.

Seeing Xolotl watching them from the corn, he said, "So this is where you got off to. Don't know how you slipped—"

"Rory," Fiona finally whispered.

Her father looked back to her, holding her by the shoulders. "What is it, love? Did your brother give you a scare or something?" He forced a chuckle, his hands still shaking. "I'm sure he didn't mean anything by it."

Fiona stared straight through him. "He took Rory."

Collin tensed. "Who took Rory, Fiona?"

"The frogman...he dragged him into the canal. Rory tried to fight him...but he was too strong...." She let out an exhausted gasp, and widened her eyes again. "Rory stopped fighting him."

Alanna covered her mouth with her hands. Collin stared at his daughter, disbelieving, but then he whispered to his wife, "Go fetch the shotgun for me."

She hurried inside, tripping on the steps. When she returned, Collin exchanged their daughter for the gun. "It's best if you and Fiona go inside, just in case." He snapped the barrel shut after making sure the weapon was loaded.

Alanna didn't move. Instead she watched her husband head for the corn.

But Xolotl cut him off. *I can't let you go and make a sacrifice of yourself.* When Collin tried to go around him, he moved over again, this time growling and raising the hair on his nape.

"Don't you growl at me, dog." He eyed Xolotl as he tried to go around yet again.

Xolotl snarled and barked, but Collin still didn't back down, so he lunged, snapping at his boots. But the butt of the shotgun greeted his face, sending him sprawling. He shook off the stunning pain, and looked around to see Collin heading into the corn. Xolotl dashed after him and this time sunk his fangs into Collin's boot, pulling back and growling.

"Let go!" Collin jabbed at him with the gun, but when Xolotl held on tight, he kicked him off. Xolotl yelped but lunged again, catching hold of Collin's calf and sinking his fangs in deep. Collin cursed, then swung the gun around and shot Xolotl in the back at close range.

The shock rendered Xolotl utterly silent and he fell over, his hind legs refusing to move. His lower body had turned into a pulpy mass of limbs and glimmering stardust. *This will take a while to heal,* he thought as he dragged himself towards the house on his front legs.

Fiona broke free of her mother and rushed to Xolotl's side as he collapsed next to the house. She buried her face in his nape and wailed. "Oh my God, Da! Look what you did to him!"

"I...I'm sorry, Fiona," her father stammered, the color drained from his face. "But he bit me—"

"He wouldn't do it without good reason," she cried.

"What in God's name is that...stuff coming out of him?" Alanna tried to yank Fiona away by the arm. "Get away from him, Fiona! He's diseased!"

At first, Fiona fought her mother off, but when she finally noticed the shimmering, golden blood, she gave up any resistance and only stared as her mother pulled her away.

Collin came to Xolotl, the expression on his face

hardening. He reloaded then squinted down the barrel sight at him. "What did you do to my son, you devil?"

"You mean this thing?" Tlaloc stood at the edge of the cornfield, holding Rory's lifeless, dripping body in his arms. He grinned past his tusk-like fangs as he tossed the boy to the ground like a sack of maize flower. "He was most filling."

Alanna fell backwards onto the porch steps, screaming.

Collin stared at his dead son a moment before turning his loathing gaze up at Tlaloc. "Demon!" He leveled the gun at him and it nearly flew out of his shaking hands when he fired.

But Tlaloc raised a water shield, slowing the buckshot so it bounced off his body as if they were soft berries instead. "Your weapon is useless, as is your life. Sacrifice the girl to me and I'll let you live."

In answer, Collin fumbled another shell into the barrel than shot at him again.

"Have it your way." Tlaloc raised his arms and a wall of water taller than the house rose up behind him.

Collin stared, dumbstruck. Fiona clung to her mother, her scream rising.

Tlaloc's smile widened. "Yes, cry for me, child. Your tears are delicious!" He threw the wall of water at them.

The wave rushed forward with a deafening roar, and it pinned Xolotl to the plank board wall. He tried to apparate away but all of his magic was focused on healing his shattered body. It tickled down his spine like army ants pressing into new territory, spreading out to his extremities with terrifying slowness. He treaded water with his good legs, trying to avoid further injury while he waited for his hind legs to work again.

The water surged with renewed power, but when he looked up, he spotted Fiona pulling herself out of the water onto the roof above him. Tlaloc hadn't gotten her yet. But both her mother and father had vanished. Another surge started a vortex that spun him around and around, pelting him with debris. He paddled hard, trying to break free of the whirlpool, but he only managed it when a wooden plank slammed him out of the funnel, injuring one of his front legs too. The clashing currents flung him up to the surface, still flailing his one good leg.

Fingers dug into the sopping fur on his shoulders and someone pulled him up by his skin. He yelped against the searing pain, and once he felt the hot tin roof under his paws, he fell over, disoriented and panicked. But when arms wrapped around his neck and he opened his one good eye to see it was Fiona, an unexpected calm settled over him. *Thank Mictlan she's safe.*

That contentment evaporated though when the house started yawning beneath them. "Dear God, what's happening?" Fiona cried.

The vortex tore into the side of the house, spitting out sideboards and splintered wood. *If I don't get us out of here now, we'll both be dead! Hurry up, stupid magic!* His hind legs began twitching, but when they turned to jerky kicks, his healing magic tapered off. *Finally!*

Fiona screamed as the house began thrashing back and forth. "We're going to die!"

"Hold on to me, and don't let go, for any reason!" he

shouted over the roar.

She crushed him in her arms, but it only lasted a breath before his magic engulfed them both and they disappeared just as the house disintegrated beneath them.

Xolotl had no idea where they were going, but when they arrived to cloudless blue skies, it hardly mattered. They'd escaped. For now.

Fiona looked around like a cornered animal. Barren desert stretched in all directions. "Mama! Da! Where are you?" she cried.

"Stop!" Xolotl shouted, his anxiety rising again. "Do you want the rain god to find us again so soon?"

She stared at him, confused.

"I'm sorry," he said, calming his own voice. "I shouldn't yell at you like that. It's just...we barely made it out of there alive."

"Where are we?"

"I don't know." Xolotl eyed the tall, sandy formations sticking out of the rocky ground. In the distance, still more shimmered in the heat. Large black birds circled overhead.

"I want to go back home!"

"Your house is gone and your family is dead. There's nothing left to go back to."

She stared at him, stricken. But then she burst into tears again.

Panicked, Xolotl tried to apparate away—*Let her fend*

for herself then!—but he reappeared only a handful of steps from where he'd stood. Between both healing himself and apparating with Fiona, he'd already expended most all of his magic. *Damn weak goat's blood.*

She hurried over. "Where are you going?"

"Apparently nowhere," he grumbled.

She sat down in the dust next to him, panting. "Please don't leave me behind! I'll do whatever you say, just please don't leave me out here all by myself."

The terror on her face brought a spike of guilt. "I won't leave you behind, but you must promise me something."

"Anything!"

"You must not cry, under any circumstances."

"Why not?"

"Because Tlaloc can smell a child's tears from miles away, and now that he's smelled yours, he will hunt you down like a coyote tracking a rabbit."

Fiona's face paled. "He's coming after me?"

Xolotl cursed himself. He'd said too much. "Don't worry. We'll find somewhere to hide." He nodded towards the mountains nearby. "We'll find some caves over there." That would hardly stop Tlaloc from finding them eventually, but at least Fiona would be out of the heat, and he could focus on regrouping.

Not that he had any hope of finding any way out of this mess without either Tlaloc or Michael sending him to sit on the Black Lake.

They started west, Xolotl keeping watch for danger. Fiona chattered non-stop, asking him all kinds of questions: "How did you learn to talk? Can you do more tricks, other than jumping all around the place like you did back there? Where did you come from? Did a witch turn you into a dog?"

At first, her talking unnerved him. The last time he'd had any substantial conversations with a human being had been hundreds of years ago, when there'd still been dead to escort to Mictlan. Under angelic rule, his kind were forbidden to talk to humans in anything other than human form, and even that was discouraged. But in truth, he missed the conversations; Lady Death was the only person who ever talked—really talked—to him anymore. It was only after the dead stopped coming that he'd realized it wasn't really the conversations he missed so much as the humans themselves.

He longed to talk to Fiona now, but fear of reprisals from the angels kept him from saying anything. And he felt bad for it. She was obviously trying not to think about what they'd just been through.

After an hour, Fiona began lagging behind in the oppressive heat. Xolotl stopped to let her catch up and rest, but she wasn't doing well on her short leg. She pressed on a good deal longer than he thought she might, but eventually she sat on a rock and declared, "I can't go on anymore." She massaged the calf muscle of her good leg, sweat glistening on her brow. Her calico blouse stuck to her body in dark, wet spots.

Xolotl paced while she rested, the lowness of the sun making him anxious. *At this rate, we won't reach the mountains by nightfall, and then we'll have to fight off the star demons.* There was only one viable option, and though it broke so many angelic rules, he'd already revealed enough about himself that he was good as dead anyway, so what did it matter? "I'm going to carry you the rest of the way." He shifted into his twisted human form.

She gasped and recoiled, and for a moment he was sure she was going to scream. Her reaction—while not surprising—disappointed him. "Do you really have the nerve to react that way to me?"

Fiona's cheeks flushed. "Sorry," she muttered. "You just...startled me, that's all."

He picked her up into his arms, taking extra care to properly balance on his backward-pointing feet, then he set off for the mountains at an awkward, loping gait.

After several minutes of silence, Fiona asked, "Were you in an accident?"

"I've always been like this," he answered, not looking at her. "Except for the eye; someone gouged that out with a bone."

"Why didn't you heal it?" When Xolotl darted a sharp glare at her, she added, "You healed yourself after Da shot you in the back, remember?"

Xolotl cracked a smile. *She certain isn't stupid.* "I can heal most wounds, but some...if they're inflicted by one of my own kind, they will scar forever."

"Was it an accident?"

He snorted. "He did it on purpose, but that's how my kind are. You think they're a friend, but you learn after a while that there is no such thing."

Fiona rode in silence a moment before saying, "Rory was always mean to me, but he'd beat up anyone who made fun of me or called me a gimp or a cripple. And then he jumped between me and that...that...." Tears threatened at her eyes.

"Try not to cry," Xolotl reminded her.

She blinked them away and nodded. "I don't want to see that...that frogman ever again."

Xolotl's job in the underworld had been to keep the dead motivated in the face of fear and pain when facing the trials, so his impulse was to assure Fiona that she wouldn't ever see Tlaloc again, to keep her from losing all hope and giving up. Yet it felt so very wrong to lie to her. After a moment's thought, he said, "If he does show up again...I will stand with you."

The shadows grew long by the time they finally reached the mountains, and Xolotl left Fiona under a shaded outcrop while he searched out a cave. He found one not far off and while she slept away the rest of the late afternoon, he went out to gather firewood. He also found a warren of rabbits, many of them sitting in the early evening shade, nibbling desert grass. After getting a fire started back in the cave, he returned to try to catch some; he needed fresh blood to rejuvenate his magic, and undoubtedly Fiona was hungry.

The rabbits proved too tricky though. He scrambled after them in dog-form, stirring them up with barks, but they soon escaped down their burrows. He leaped after the last one but rammed head-first into the rock over the hole just as the rabbit slipped past him. He shook his head, mending the twinge in his neck, then set to digging up the burrow. Finding nothing, he soon gave up.

And he felt watched. He scanned the mountainside, ears alert and his divine senses extending, but they came back with nothing. The feeling intensified though, so Xolotl headed off south, following a crude track around the bend, to the western slope of the mountain.

In the day's dying light he spotted a coyote pawing at something moving along the ground. It tried to bite the creature's tall, rounded back, but its prey reward it by jumping into the air and smacking the coyote's lower jaw. The coyote shook its head but then continued the pursuit through the grass. Curious, Xolotl trotted out to investigate.

The coyote raised its head and growled. When Xolotl didn't stop, it looked around then barked a sharp warning.

Xolotl changed into his human-form and raised his hands above his head. "Away with you, stupid trickster!"

The coyote took off running, but stopped a distance away to look back, tongue hanging out.

Xolotl changed back again and followed the scurrying creature through the brush. It headed for a burrow among the yucca, so he leaped to block the entrance. He morphed back into a human and scooped up the leathery creature, holding it firmly as it wriggled. An armadillo. "Too bad you have no hands, coyote," he laughed, holding up his prize. He then limped back the way he'd come, holding the squealing, clawing animal out in front of him.

Back in the shade, he sat down. His treasure stared back at him with wide, black eyes, sniffing at him with a long, armor-plated nose and beating against his arm with its tail. The underside was soft, so he brought back his dog-head and tore open its throat with his teeth. He lapped up the bubbling blood, luxuriating in the tingling of rebuilding magic, and once the creature stopped struggling, he went back to his human head and sucked the rest out. "Ahhhh!" Now if only he could find a dozen more armadillos—

"Enjoying yourself, Xolotl?"

Xolotl turned to see the angel Raphael perched like a vulture on the rocky outcrop above him. He wore modern clothing—shirt, pants, an overcoat, even leather boots—and a knife sheath hung from his belt.

Xolotl dropped the dead armadillo, hands trembling. He bowed his head, avoiding eye contact as he muttered, "My Lord."

"Do you know where I just came from?" Raphael asked.

After a tense swallow, Xolotl said, "I don't, My Lord."

Raphael pointed to the east. "A little town a ways over the horizon back there, at a farm house that inexplicably experienced a devastating flashflood in the middle of a cloudless, sunny summer day, leaving three humans dead. That's awfully strange, don't you think?"

Xolotl hunched lower, drawing his twisted body in upon itself. "Strange indeed, My Lord."

"The scene bares all the hallmarks of an act by the rain god. You don't know anything about that, do you?"

When Xolotl fumbled over his words, Raphael jumped down and alit to stand in front of him. He bent down, and said, his voice low, "Have I not always been fair with you and your master?"

"You have," Xolotl admitted, still not looking up.

"We both saw the rain god sitting dead on the banks of the Black Lake not two days ago, but now he's roaming the New Mexico territory? How can that be?"

Xolotl squeezed his eye shut and clutched at his greasy hair. "It was an accident! I was trying to get them all back to Mictlan before anyone noticed, but things with Tlaloc went terribly wrong!"

Raphael recoiled, his eyes wide. "What do you mean by 'them'? How many others are out there now?"

After a trembling sob, Xolotl admitted, "All of them." He curled into a ball, awaiting the kick.

But Raphael strode away, his feathers ruffled as he paced, muttering under his breath. But then he stopped and turned back to Xolotl, a shadow of fear in his eyes. "Even Smoking Mirror?"

Xolotl nodded.

Raphael exhaled hard. "This is not good. Not good at all."

"Please have mercy, My Lord! I was trying to take Tlaloc back to Mictlan, but then the children came, and he saw them.... I didn't want any of that to happen, My Lord! I got the girl out as fast as I could—"

"You have a human child with you?" Raphael asked, surprised.

"I couldn't leave her there, My Lord. Tlaloc would have

fed on her."

Raphael went back to silent contemplation while Xolotl waited, clutching the dead armadillo to his chest. Eventually, Raphael turned around again. "Well, what's done is done, but things aren't out of control yet. If I understand Tlaloc's appetites correctly, he's probably still seeking the girl you rescued."

"Once he tastes a child's tears, he won't stop looking for her."

"Then it shouldn't be too difficult to lure him here, to deal with him."

"I haven't the power to deal with a god of his magical skill. I was to bring the revived gods back to Mictlan before they regained their memories, for Lord Death to deal with himself. I have very little real power of my own."

"That's why I'll deal with him myself," Raphael said.

Overcome with relief, Xolotl prostrated himself on the ground at the angel's feet. "You're most merciful, My Lord!"

Raphael stepped away, disgusted. "Get up already. We have a vicious god to deal with, and it's already getting dark."

But Xolotl shook his head. "We should wait until morning."

"Time is of the essence, Black Dog."

"It is, but the child is in no condition to resist another attack right now. And the Tzitzimime prowl the dark again. With the late moonrise, they'll be out seeking sustenance in preparation for their mistress's return. Our best chance for success is in daylight, when we need only worry about the one danger."

Raphael looked back at the western horizon where the sun had already sunk, chased away by the coming twilight. "Then we'll meet here again in the morning, at first light. Once I've dealt with Tlaloc, we'll discuss how we're going to wrangle up the rest of them."

Xolotl stared down at the armadillo. "And once we've recaptured all of them...what will you tell Michael?"

"If everything goes well, he need not ever know."

Xolotl cast a confused gaze up at Raphael's back but didn't dare question.

"Tomorrow morning." With a curt nod, Raphael took to wing, soon vanishing into the growing twilight.

Morphing back into a dog, Xolotl hurried back to the cave to find Fiona huddled in the back corner. A look of relief spread over her face when she saw him. "I didn't think you were coming back."

"I said I wouldn't abandon you, and I won't." He dropped the armadillo into her lap. "I would have been back sooner, but I encountered some trouble getting dinner." He changed back into his human form and sat next to the fire too. When she just stared at the dead animal in her lap, he said, "Eat up."

Fiona wrinkled her nose. "I can't eat it like this. It's raw."

"So?"

"It has to be cooked. Mama says you must cook meat all the way through or it'll make you sick."

"Put it in the fire then."

"But it must be gutted first or it will spoil the meat."

Xolotl took the armadillo, changed into his dog-head then used his fangs as knives to cut the belly open. When he started tearing the innards out with his mouth, Fiona cried in disgust. "What?" he asked, bits of entrails tumbling from his mouth as he did.

"That's so gross!"

He spit out the rest, feeling sheepish, and finished the job with his hands. He set the armadillo belly-down in the fire.

"Mama used to make the best dinners," Fiona commented as the cave filled with the aroma of cooking meat. "Bacon and cabbage, and skirts and kidneys. Her soda bread was wonderful and she made a glorious Christmas haddock, though not as good as my grandmama's. Still, what with the creamed peas and potatoes...oh, you would have loved it!"

"I don't eat flesh, cooked or otherwise," Xolotl said.

"Then what do you eat?"

"Blood, mostly."

"Are you a vampire then? Your skin is kind of green."

Xolotl laughed. "Not all things that feed on blood are undead. Besides, where I come from, only noble women who die in childbirth become vampires."

"Where are you from?"

He hesitated before replying, "Mexico."

"Is it pretty down there?"

"There is no place more beautiful, even if the Spanish ruined much of it when they came grubbing for the gold. It's strange how a useless metal can so easily bewitch the human mind."

Fiona nodded. "Da talked about moving to California when they found gold out there. He even went for a couple months, but he said it wasn't any place for women and children, so we stayed in Texas instead." She poked at the armadillo with a stick. "What's going to happen to me now?"

He hadn't thought about that. With so many other things on his mind, it was easy to forget that she had no home left to go back to. "I don't know yet, but we'll figure it out soon."

Once the armadillo finished cooking, Fiona scraped the meat out with a sharp rock and used the shell for a bowl. "Are you sure you don't want any?"

"Like I said, I eat only blood. And sometimes insects."

She cringed. "You really eat bugs?"

He smiled. "The ones my master makes...they are simply divine. I love how the centipedes' skittering legs tickle my tongue, or how the spiders' hairy, soft bodies explode when I bite down on them." He sighed, a little ache forming in his chest. "Lady Death used to wrap them in tortillas for me, as if hosting dinner guests were a perfectly natural...thing...to...."

"Are you all right?" Fiona asked, concern on her face.

He shook his head, clearing the fuzziness. "I'm fine."

"You looked like you were going to fall asleep."

"I don't sleep."

"I wish I didn't have to. I'm pretty sure I miss out on a lot of exciting things when I'm asleep."

Xolotl chuckled.

Once Fiona finished eating, she sat staring into the fire. Outside, the star demons howled and hissed; some even ventured close enough to the cave to see their red eyes glowing in the dark. She hugged her knees to her chest, quaking. "What are they?"

"Don't worry about them. They can't come near the firelight, for it will burn them." He just hoped he'd gathered enough firewood to last them through the night.

Fiona yawned but continued watching the cave mouth.

"You should get to sleep," Xolotl suggested. "Tomorrow comes all too quickly."

She cast an imploring gaze over at him.

"Don't worry. I'll make sure the fire burns all night."

When she still didn't look away, he smiled back and looked away himself, uncomfortable. *Why is she staring at me?*

"Can I sleep in your lap?" she finally piped up.

He blinked at her, taken aback. "Why?"

"The floor is too hard...and your lap would be a lot more comfortable."

Xolotl eyed her. Such a strange child; he'd never met a human—dead or alive—who wanted to be touched by him, not even to accept a helping hand when climbing the steep trails of the mountain of obsidian blades in Mictlan. Understandable, since he looked dead himself, and he used to mark the living for death by licking them.

"It's all right," Fiona said when he didn't say anything.

"I'm sure the floor will be just fine." She went back to staring into the fire, her gaze occasionally wandering to the cave mouth.

Shaking his head, he said, "If it will help you sleep—"

She hurried over and settled onto his lap before he could finish. He stiffened though when she drew his arms around her like a blanket. "When I was younger, Da would let me sit in his lap until I fell asleep," she murmured. "He used to sing me a lullaby in his native Irish." She squeezed her eyes shut and frowned.

"I don't know any Irish songs," Xolotl said, the whole conversation proving awkward for him. "Nor can I really sing at all."

She set her ear against his chest, listening. "I can't hear your heartbeat."

"I don't have a heart."

"But how can that be?"

"My kind don't have such things...well, not most of us, anyway. It's not something we're created with."

"But you can get one?"

"A few have, but it doesn't really do anything useful." If anything, a divine heart made gods treacherous, like Quetzalcoatl.

"But if it does nothing useful, why would anyone get one? That makes no sense."

Xolotl sighed. "I don't know why, they just do. Now off to sleep with you. Tomorrow will be a big day."

"What's tomorrow?"

Quite possibly the last day of our lives. But he kept the thought to himself. He hugged her a little tighter. He wasn't sure why he did it, but it made him feel better.

But it also confused him. His job—his entire existence—was to care for the dead, not the living, and yet here he sat, trying to figure out how he was going to do the impossible: keep her from dying tomorrow.

Fiona slept past sunrise, even after Xolotl laid her on the ground so he could sit at the mouth of the cave in his dog-form, waiting for Raphael and watching gray clouds moving in from the east. "Is that you, Tlaloc?" he whispered, anxious. The angel was supposed to be here already. *Just like stupid angels to take their own damn time at others' expense.* By the time he roused Fiona, he was in a foul mood.

She stared at him bleary-eyed and confused but then gave him a sleepy smile. "Good morning, Travis."

He scowled at her. "My name is Xolotl."

She giggled. "That's a funny name."

"Not any funnier than yours."

Her smile faded. "I'm sorry. I wasn't making fun."

Xolotl returned to the cave mouth to scan the skies some more. Where in Mictlan was Raphael?

She joined him. "What's wrong?"

"Nothing."

"You're upset about something."

"It's nothing you can help me with."

"I could try."

Xolotl raised a lip at her. "You've done enough already,

thank you."

She blinked. "What's that mean?"

"Nothing." He trotted down the trail, to where he'd met the angel last night. Raphael wasn't there either. Blast him!

Fiona came up behind him. "Why are you mad me?"

He ignored her, heading back to the cave.

But she stomped her foot. "Why are you suddenly being so mean? What did I do?"

He rounded on her, shaking. "Everything! Tlaloc is coming to kill you, and I don't know that I can stop him! If you'd just listened to me yesterday by the canal, neither of us would be in this predicament! Why didn't you listen to me? Why did you call your brother over? Why didn't you go back to the house like I told you to?"

Her breathing had grown more labored with each question, and now she stared at him, bewildered. "You mean because of me...my brother and my parents are dead?"

Xolotl snapped his mouth shut. "Fiona, no, that's not—" he started but when the tears welled in her eyes, he morphed back into his man-form and gripped her shoulders with both hands. "I don't mean that at all. Please, don't cry. I'm sorry; I let my anger get the better of me—"

"They *are* dead because of me!" She shrugged him off and lumbered off down the path, her sobs echoing through the canyon.

"Fiona! Come back! You can't go off on your own! Tlaloc might be out there right now!" He started after her, but fell on his face within five steps and nearly went down the side of the rocky hill. He looked around, dazed and bleeding stardust from fresh wounds.

Fiona was gone.

I must find her, before Tlaloc does! He morphed into his hound-form and limped the rest of the way down the path until his wounds healed themselves. He then took to a full-out run down into the sandy spires below.

But when he turned the first corner into the rock formations, he ran headlong into Tlaloc, knocking himself backwards.

The rain god held Fiona, hugging her with one arm while covering her mouth with the other hand. "So smart of you to keep watch over my sacrifice while I regrouped," Tlaloc said with a tusk-filled smile. "Maybe I'll spare you yet, Black Dog."

Xolotl looked to the sky, praying he'd see Raphael swooping down at them, but he saw only roiling black and gray clouds overhead.

"And a good thing I found you when I did, for I am famished!" Tlaloc uncovered Fiona's mouth but before she could scream, he jammed his fingers into her mouth, gagging her. Water drizzled out her nose and her eyes rolled up into her head, her body going into convulsions.

Without hesitation, Xolotl leaped and buried his fangs into Tlaloc's hand, dragging it out of Fiona's mouth. She vomited water then broke into shrill screams, but Tlaloc didn't release her. Roaring, he tried to tear his hand back but Xolotl held on, even as Tlaloc flung him back and forth. "Release me, Black Dog!"

But Xolotl clamped down harder.

Finally letting Fiona go, Tlaloc turned his full attention on Xolotl. "You truly *are* as stupid as everyone says!" He punched Xolotl upside the head. "How dare you even touch me?"

When the fifth hit sent stardust spurting from his nose, Xolotl finally let go. He stumbled a few steps, disoriented, but when he saw Tlaloc advancing on Fiona—who was bent over on all fours, still coughing up water—he lunged and grabbed hold of Tlaloc's bare ankle, taking his feet out from under him. Tlaloc hit the ground with a grunt.

Fiona looked over her shoulder at them, her eyes wide with panic. Tlaloc clawed towards her, so she scrambled away up the side of the hill, towards a nest of boulders.

Tlaloc roared, bringing thunder with it. He rolled over and kicked Xolotl in the face so hard Xolotl lost his canine form. Tlaloc pounced on him, pinning him to the ground on his back. "Treacherous dog! You wish to be dealt with first? Then let's do it your way."

Xolotl tried to push him off, but Tlaloc dug his knees into his arms, rendering them useless. Panicked, Xolotl morphed back into a dog and snapped ferociously at Tlaloc's hands.

But Tlaloc grabbed his muzzle and clamped it shut. "You like being a dog so much...then you can die like one!" He pressed his free hand against Xolotl's chest with crushing force.

Pain and a strange burning sensation spread through him. *Apparate! Apparate!*—a last-ditch and extremely dangerous option: taking Tlaloc with him into the in-between—where all magic flowed like a river to anywhere in the world—would render him completely vulnerable to an attack that could completely obliterate him, but he had to risk it.

But his magic turned to sludge inside him. Thudding that started in his chest below Tlaloc's hand soon turned to pounding in his ears, growing quicker and more erratic with each second. *What is happening to me?* He tried to apparate yet again but he felt only a strange rushing sensation completely unlike any magic he'd ever experienced.

"You're as treacherous as that sniveling, whining Feathered Serpent," Tlaloc snarled then punched Xolotl across the face. The pain exploded through Xolotl's head, and everything went black.

When the world came back, Tlaloc still loomed over him, and a deliciously familiar metallic taste filled his mouth. *Blood?* The pounding in his head intensified when he noticed the smear of crimson on Tlaloc's knuckles. *Mictlan save me! Did he just turn me mortal?*

"We all should have done away with Quetzalcoatl when we had the chance, but you...I won't make that mistake with you." Tlaloc raised both hands to the sky, bringing lightning flashes and rumbling thunder with the rain pelting down from the sky.

The ground turned to mud and more flowed down the canyon walls in rivers, turning the desert floor into a silt-filled soup. It soaked into Xolotl's fur and crawled into his ears. As it rose higher, his efforts to wiggle free turned from determined to panicked, but the rain god held fast.

Tlaloc shoved his head down into the mud until all he heard was his new heart dancing drunkenly in his ears. The mud oozed into his nostrils but he resisted the urge to draw in breath. *Omeyocan save me! He's going to drown me!*

And unlike the other gods, there would be no sitting on the Black Lake waiting for Lord Death to resurrect him; he wasn't a god anymore, just a mortal, and not even a human. Humans might look forward to eternal bliss in one of the many heavens if they gave their life in sacrifice to the gods, but animals just disappeared, ceased to exist altogether....

He was going to truly, and finally, die.

But suddenly Tlaloc let him go.

Xolotl thrashed to the surface then gasped for breath, his chest burning. Air had never tasted so wonderful. Disoriented, he swam to the nearest rock shelf and climbed out of the rising mud, his legs trembling under the thick weight of his muddy coat. He shook it off, nearly falling back into the sludge below him, but then he looked around.

Fiona stood on a high overhang, pelting the rain god with rocks as he scaled the mountain towards her.

"Run!" Xolotl shouted, but to his surprise, only a bark came out.

"Leave him alone, you monster!" Fiona threw another rock, this time clipping Tlaloc's forehead. He bellowed curses at her and didn't stop, but she held her ground. "You keep coming, you damn frogman! I'm not afraid of you!"

Death's Good Dog

Xolotl bounded up the mountain side, pressing his muscles hard in spite of their protesting. He grabbed Tlaloc's ankle again and began pulling him back down.

Tlaloc gripped onto a boulder with both webbed hands. "Get off me, you two-face dog!" He kicked but Xolotl dodged it.

"Get him, Xolotl! Get him!" Fiona chucked another rock, and this one shattered the stone rim of Tlaloc's water-filled goggles on the left side. "That's for Rory, you devil!"

The rain god clutched at his broken goggle and shrieked, surprised. When he pulled his hand away, he glared up at her with a shriveled eye. "You'll pay for that, you little bitch!" He grabbed Xolotl by his scruff.

Xolotl tried to hold onto Tlaloc's ankle, but the rain god hauled him up over his head, tearing loose divine flesh. Xolotl yelped as Tlaloc lobbed him like a rock up at Fiona.

She tried to scramble aside but Xolotl bowled her over, sending her feet out from under her, and she nearly went over the edge of the overhang. She caught the lip with her elbows and held on. "Help! I can't hold on!"

"You don't need too." Tlaloc seized her good leg.

She nearly lost her grip but Xolotl snapped up her dress collar and pulled back.

Tlaloc bared his tusk-fangs and yanked harder.

Fiona squealed but then kicked him in the face with her shorter leg. The blow connected with the rain god's remaining goggle. He grunted and tried to swat her foot away, but she kicked back even harder, over and over.

"Let...go...of me...you...beast!"

The last strike broke the seal on the stone goggle and Tlaloc shrieked, clutching at his face with both hands. Xolotl pulled Fiona up the rest of the way.

Tlaloc squinted up at them through his one half-full goggle. "You've earned yourself a slow, torturous death, girl!" He then clawed his way up onto the ledge, and crouched, shaking his head back and forth to keep the water on his eye.

Fiona retreated to the cliff wall, searching for an escape, but there was nowhere left to go.

I must take out that goggle for good, Xolotl decided and he sprang atop Tlaloc, snapping at his face. He clanked his teeth on the goggle's stone rim, radiating pain through his head, but with the next bite, he found his grip and started pulling and twisting.

Tlaloc stepped backwards over the edge, bashing at him with both hands, and cursing and shrieking. They tumbled head over feet down the hill, hitting rocks, tearing up scrub brush, and burying themselves in a thick coat of mud. When they finally hit the bottom, the flesh holding Tlaloc's goggles in place gave way with a ripping *pop!*

The rain god clawed at his face. "My eyes! My eyes!"

Xolotl danced away, clutching the goggles in his mouth like a hard-won trophy. *We just might make it out of this!* He turned his gaze up to Fiona and wagged his tail, elated.

"Oh no! Look out!" Fiona cried from up above. "Behind you!"

He looked back in time to see Tlaloc heave a chunk of boulder at him.

Xolotl leaped but too late; the rock landed on his left hind leg, crushing bones and pulling him down into the sloppy mud. He yelped and cried, yanking with all of his might to get free, but flames of pain raced up his leg.

Tlaloc's grotesque face appeared over the boulder, his black eyes shriveled to pinpoints above his snarl. "Well played, Black Dog. You managed to blind me, but you still lose." He seized Xolotl by the throat and squeezed.

Xolotl pawed at him, his eye bulging with the building pressure. He heard screaming, but his stare remained fixed on Tlaloc's enraged face. *What will become of Fiona? Who will take care of her? Who's going to keep her safe from Tlaloc?*

But as the darkness descended, strange sounds rushed in on his ears: thunder, wings flapping, singeing metal, crackling flames. And his name being called over and over again.

The first thing he saw when his vision returned was Tlaloc's head lying on the ground in front of him. The rest lay off to the side, twitching. Raphael stood between the two, his arms outstretched, a flaming gold-sword in his right hand. The angel's face though...it wasn't fury or bloodlust he saw there, but rather surprise...and regret. He breathed heavily.

Tlaloc's body slowly melted into a puddle of water, and

overhead, the black rain clouds dissolved, revealing clear blue sky.

Raphael sheathed his sword in the knife sheath at his hip then leaned over Xolotl. He touched his nose then rubbed the blood between his fingers. "Well, that's unfortunate." But when a rock hit him in the back of the head, he raised his wings to shield himself. He massaged the back of his head as he turned to see who had attacked him.

Fiona stumbled down the side of the mountain, pausing every couple of steps to scoop up a muddy rock to throw at Raphael. "Get away from him, you ugly turkey vulture!"

Raphael batted the stones away, perturbed. "I'm here to help, not hurt him, so stop already."

She narrowed her eyes but lowered the next stone ready in her hand. "You're an angel, aren't you? Like the priests talk about in church?"

He half-heartedly glared at her. "I should have known you'd be nearby. Too late to put my wings away now."

She glared right back at him. "I asked you a question."

"Yes, I'm an angel."

"And you say you're here to help him? Then get to helping him already!"

"Yes, Archangel, sir."

"What's that to mean?"

Raphael shook his head but a smile slipped onto his lips. He turned to examine the boulder then carefully lifted it off Xolotl's foot.

Fiona hurried to the bottom of the hill and slid to her

knees in the mud next to Xolotl. "Everything will be all right, Xolotl," she whispered, stroking his head to calm him. To Raphael, she asked, "Can you fix him?"

"Healing happens to be my specialty." Raphael set his hands on Xolotl's wounded haunch.

Touching the broken leg felt little different than setting fire to it. Xolotl's every instinct told him to get away, but his body was too exhausted and bruised to follow through; he could only manage to bury his head in Fiona's lap, the world threatening to black out again.

"Just another moment," Raphael murmured, kneading his fingers into the muscle.

Finally a cool, soothing magic poured through Xolotl's flesh, extinguishing the hundreds of fires torturing his leg. It traveled slowly at first but then spread through the rest of his body, chasing away the aches and stings. He sighed in relief. And curiously, his tail started wagging of its own volition.

"You fixed his leg completely! It's good as new!" Fiona said.

Raphael nodded.

She ran her fingers over Xolotl's newly healed leg. "Can you do the same...for me?"

"There's something wrong with your leg too?"

"One of them is shorter than the other."

A look of pity crossed Raphael's face. "That's the way God made you, child."

Fiona bit her lip and nodded. After a tense pause, she muttered, "That's not real Christian of Him, making some of us suffer just because 'that's the way He made you'."

Raphael turned his gaze away, uncomfortable. "Unfortunately, I've done all I can do for this one." He removed his hands from Xolotl's leg.

"What else is wrong with him?" When Raphael hesitated to answer, Fiona asked Xolotl, "Does it still hurt somewhere?"

Xolotl looked up at her and whined.

She frowned until the truth hit her. "What happened to his voice? He used to be able to talk. And he could change into a man; not a handsome one, like my Da, but a good man anyway."

"He can't do that anymore." Raphael stood, flexing his wings in agitation. "His...friend turned him into a real dog, and I haven't the power to undo that. Only the one who did it can, and I just sent him back where to he came from."

"Then bring him back here, so he can fix him!"

"Not an option."

"Then what about God? Mama always said the Good Lord could do anything."

Raphael laughed. "Trust me, you don't want to involve my father. We're better leaving him out of this."

"But you can't leave him like this," Fiona cried. "He...he's a pretty good dog and all, but he's not supposed to be one."

Raphael stared down at Xolotl, chewing the inside of his lip thoughtfully. "This does complicate matters. Do you have some shelter near here? He needs to get out of the sun."

Death's Good Dog

✡

Fiona led the way back to the cave while Raphael carried Xolotl's limp body. He set him down next to the remains of the fire pit, and when Xolotl tried to get up, dizziness kept him from even rolling off his side. His gut ached with a strange unpleasantness. *What is wrong with me?* he tried to ask, but he could only whine and yip. He stared at Raphael imploringly.

Raphael shook his head. "I don't speak your new language, Black Dog."

"I bet he's hungry," Fiona said. "We should find something for him to eat."

The angel nodded. "A good idea. What do dogs eat?"

She shrugged. "Scraps mostly, but you won't find any around here. He brought me an armadillo for dinner last night though."

"Then go get one."

"I'm not going out there alone." She looked at the cave mouth anxiously. "What if that...that frogman comes back again?"

"He won't. He's dead." Seeing the hesitation in her eyes, he sighed. "Very well, I'll go with you."

She picked up the empty armadillo shell. "We should bring some water too, before the puddles dry up."

Raphael checked the sword at his hip. "I know nothing about eating or drinking, so you lead the way."

Fiona kissed Xolotl on the forehead. "Don't worry. We'll be back with something good to eat, and you'll feel much better with a full belly."

Xolotl thumped his tail in thanks, but once they left, he curled up, making himself as small as possible, hiding his head and welcoming the strangely contenting darkness when it swept over him again. Anything was better than thinking about the truth of his situation.

Xolotl walked towards the Black Lake, the reeds clattering like dried bones as he pushed through. No gods sat on the banks, not even Tlaloc, but even stranger, no ghost lights hummed through the air like lightning bugs. The silence pressed in like a heavy weight.

He went to the palace to speak with his master, but Lord Death wasn't there either. He searched the cenote's caverns for Lady Death but she too was gone, and all of her trinkets, mats, and weavings had faded to dusty gray. Her jars of magic insects sat empty too. "Master!" he shouted, his voice echoing in the emptiness. "Please come out! Please don't leave me alone like this!"

But no one answered.

Someone pushed his shoulder and suddenly he was back in the cave, his body as heavy as a sack of stones. The air smelled wonderful but his mouth felt sticky and dry. *What new torture is this?*

"Here, try drinking this." Fiona pushed him up onto his belly and set the armadillo shell between his feet. "The food's almost ready."

He grunted but drank, slowly at first but then with more urgency. He'd never tasted anything so wonderful, and to his relief it took the edge off the pain in his gut and moistened his dry throat. He finished the bowl, licking as much as he could off the sides before Fiona took it away. "I'll get some more." She then hurried from the cave.

Raphael sat next to the fire, gutting a rabbit carefully with his flaming sword. A spit cobbled together from tree limbs sat over the fire, and a skinned rabbit was already roasting over the flames. He frowned in disgust as he chucked a handful of offal out of the cave mouth.

Xolotl crawled across the floor towards the fire, following his nose.

"I wouldn't get too close," Raphael warned. "This is already taking more time than I'd like, so I'd rather not have to heal you from burns too."

Xolotl snorted but stopped his advance, watching the rabbit sizzle. The longer he watched, the more his belly gurgled and complained.

Fiona returned with another shell full of water, walking carefully as not to spill. While Xolotl drank it down, she turned the rabbit and occasionally pulled the spit off to poke at the meat with her fingers. Once she decided it was finished, she had Raphael slice it off the bones with his sword then she fed it to Xolotl a bit at a time. He gobbled down each piece, not bothering with chewing before looking for the next. Several times he tried to grab the carcass from her, but she pulled it out of his reach. "You could choke on the bones," she scolded him. "Don't worry, I won't let you starve."

Once the second rabbit was cooked, she picked off that

carcass too, though by then the disturbing ache in his gut was mostly gone. She ate some too but gave most of it to him.

Once the last of the meat was gone, and his belly was full, he felt strong enough to try walking again. Fiona walked with him, straddling his back so she could catch him if he floundered, but after he got his muscles warmed, he moved with little trouble.

"Finally we can get underway." Raphael had been watching from outside the cave while they ate and now took to pacing. "At this rate we'll be lucky to make it to the presidio by nightfall."

"What's at the presidio?" Fiona asked as she dumped mud onto the remains of the fire.

"There's a church there, and the priests will take you in now that your parents are dead."

"I suppose that'll be all right." She ruffled Xolotl's ears. "They'll take good care of us."

"He's not coming with us."

"Not coming—?" She cast a questioning glance at Raphael but then drew Xolotl into her arms. "No. I won't go without him!"

Raphael rubbed his forehead. "No matter how much he looks like a dog, child, he's not one, and the priests will soon start to suspect there's something wrong with him."

"There's nothing wrong with him! If anything, you're the wrong one! He might not be a real dog, but he's a darn good one!"

Her words spread a welcome warmth through Xolotl's chest. He wagged his tail and whined, nudging up against her cheek with his nose.

Raphael chuckled. "Ah yes, Death's good dog. You should listen to yourself; have you any idea what this *dog* used to do before my kind came and saved humanity from his kind? He used to make the dead go through horrible, painful trials, all for the promise of eternal peace, but in fact it was all a ploy to feed their immortal souls to his master."

Xolotl growled. *Untrue! I helped the dead conquer the trials; I made sure they didn't languish in limbo forever, suffering and fearful. And Lord Death eats their hearts, not their souls, you liar!* He started barking, too frustrated to keep his anger in anymore. *Liar!*

Fiona hugged him tighter. "I don't believe you," she told Raphael.

"Yes, well, you nearly found out how wrong you are; your 'frogman' used to be sitting dead in the underworld until your friend here brought him—and all the rest of their brutish kind—back from the dead, and unleashed them on the world again. Tlaloc isn't even the most powerful of them, and he nearly killed him. That's just one god driven by his instinct to eat. Some of these others…they are driven by far more dangerous hungers, for power, and destruction, and total domination. That, child, is what *he* released on this world." He jabbed his finger at Xolotl.

Fiona looked down at Xolotl, awe in her eyes. "You're a god?"

Xolotl glanced over at Raphael, who now stood stalk still as her words sank in. When he met Xolotl's gaze, he bristled. "Now you've made me admit—in front of a good Catholic, of all things—!" He stopped, gritting his teeth and wiping his hand over his face. "Christ! I should have turned you over to Michael in the first place! If Michael finds out that I...brother or no brother, he'll kill me!" He took to pacing again. "What am I going to do?"

Xolotl wriggled free of Fiona then picked up a small stick from the firewood pile. He went to the mouth of the cave and started dragging the stick through the thick layer of dirt and dust there, drawing patterns.

Raphael paused to watch him, and Fiona came over to see what he was doing as well. "What's he making?" she asked.

"He's writing, in his people's language."

"What does it say?"

"I don't know. It's too messy to read."

Xolotl snorted then tried again, going slower this time, to make sure his markings were legible.

"Your mission?" Raphael asked, his brow furrowed.

Xolotl nodded.

"He has a mission?" Fiona asked.

After a hesitation, Raphael sighed then answered, "He's supposed to find all the gods he resurrected and return them to the underworld before the Archangel finds out they're missing. I never should have agreed to it to start with, but now...there is no other good choice, not if I don't want my wings cut off."

Xolotl nodded again.

"But...but he has no magic anymore!" Fiona said. "The frogman nearly killed him, and if the others are worse than him...." She looked at Xolotl, fear shimmering in her eyes.

"I will help him," Raphael assured her. "He'll hunt them down, and I will take care of them." He tapped his finger on his chin as he scrutinized Xolotl. "Though it will look very suspicious if I'm away from the Kingdom for so long, tagging along after a dog...."

After a moment's thought, he reached over his back and plucked a feather, seemingly from the air itself, since he'd hidden his wings away. He mashed the feather between his hands, rubbing them together as if forming a ball with a piece of clay. When he finished, a bright auburn-colored gemstone sat on his palm. He knelt and beckoned Xolotl to him. "Open your mouth."

Xolotl hesitated but then obeyed. Raphael set the gemstone on the tip of his index finger than pressed it against the back of Xolotl's left front canine tooth. Heat spread through the tooth, radiating into his jaw, but it stopped as soon as Raphael withdrew his finger. Xolotl felt the back of his tooth with his tongue. The small smooth stone now stuck out of the back of it.

"The gem's magic is triggered by divine blood, so when you come upon one of the other gods, you need only bite them and it will alert me," Raphael said.

Like you did today? Xolotl curled his lip.

Perhaps sensing Xolotl's sentiment, if not his actual thoughts, Raphael added, "Just remember that I might not always be able to come immediately without drawing attention, so get yourself away from the scene as soon as you can. You're no use to anyone dead." He stood again.

"It's time for us to part ways. Remember, the sooner we finish this, the safer our secret will be, and...once they're all back on the Black Lake where they belong, I'll raise Tlaloc just long enough to make him take this curse off you."

Xolotl wasn't sure he could trust the angel's promise—they were treacherous creatures—but what choice did he have? He wagged his tail in thanks, if only to maintain politeness.

"Now, you get tracking our next target while I take the girl to the presidio."

But Fiona folded her arms. "And like I said before, I'm not going anywhere. Xolotl's going to need help on this mission, especially since you can't bother sticking around to make sure he doesn't get killed."

"You would hardly qualify as help, child," Raphael replied. "It's only by dumb luck that you're alive now."

"Well, it seems to me that Xolotl is only stuck as a dog because you're slow as molasses," Fiona fired back. "And don't try to say that you just happened by and stopped all this; I might have a bum leg, but that doesn't make me stupid. Besides, I owe him."

Raphael laughed. "Owe him? Your family is dead because of him!"

"Maybe, but he didn't plan that. He tried to run me off, tried to warn me...." She clenched her jaw, fighting back tears. Eventually she found her voice again. "He didn't intend any of that to happen, but when that monster came for me today...he put himself between me and it, knowing full-well it would mean his own death, but he did it anyway. I'm alive because of him, and so I owe him my life." She smiled tightly at Xolotl.

Xolotl wanted to tell her, *It's all right to cry now, Fiona. It's safe,* but all he could do was nudge up against her leg and whine.

Raphael's face fell into a pitying frown. "That may be, but this is a very dangerous task, and with that leg of yours—"

"Mamma taught me to never let it stop me from doing anything, and I won't let it start now," she answered. When the angel still didn't look convinced, she added, "If you make me go to that presidio of yours, I'll tell everyone what I saw here, and that Saint Raphael told me that God isn't the only god."

He flinched, taken aback. "I didn't tell you my name."

She gave him a smug grin. "Mamma taught me all about the saints, and you said healing is your special gift, so it wasn't too hard to figure out. Maybe the priests won't believe me at first, but after a while, if I keep at them, they just might start praying on it, and then that Archangel you keep going on about might catch wind—"

"All right, all right! You can go with him!" Raphael frowned. "But if you get killed, that's on you—and *him.*" He pointed at Xolotl.

Fiona smiled. "I'm fine with that, thank you."

Xolotl nudged her hand with his nose and wagged his tail. *Don't worry. Taking care of humans on dangerous journeys is what I do best.*

"And since he can't tell you this stuff himself, I will fully brief you on this mission, so you know what you're getting into." Raphael knelt and motioned them to him. "There are dozens of these gods that need to be dealt with, but there are certain ones that should be your first priority; the sooner they're returned to Mictlan, the better, for everyone.

"The goddess Coyolxauhqui: she's a powerful sorceress who controls night demons and uses her magic to bewitch entire towns to her dark ambitions. Luckily, she'll likely be distracted by her brother, so you might be able to use their quarreling to your advantage. But her brother Mextli...be very, very cautious. Whereas his sister bewitches hundreds of people, he's as likely to butcher just as many—and more—to eat their hearts. And their mother, Coatlicue, isn't much better than her children; she controls an army of undead women, not just to collect her blood sacrifices, but to also serve as her body guards. She will be very difficult to get to."

"Sounds hard," Fiona admitted, fidgeting but still maintaining her steely resolve.

"They're not the ones to truly worry about." Raphael turned his gaze squarely on Xolotl. "You must find Smoking Mirror before he gets his memory back; if he remembers who he is and what he's capable of...I don't know that even I could stop him. We both know what he did to Michael when they last battled."

Xolotl nodded, his expression grave.

"What did he do to him?" Fiona asked.

"That's not your concern," Raphael replied, his tone a clipped warning. "Suffice it to say that our father—even as all-powerful as he is—couldn't fully heal his injuries."

Fiona swallowed hard, doubt on her face. But when Raphael asked if she'd changed her mind, she scowled. "I'm not afraid!"

He glared at her. "You should be. Very much so." He stood and unfurled his massive golden-brown wings again. "I must go; there are war council meetings today and Michael frowns on tardiness." To Xolotl, he added, "Find Smoking Mirror, and soon. Make him your top priority." He ducked outside and disappeared with a handful of massive wing flaps.

Fiona went to the entrance to watch him fade from sight in the sky. Xolotl joined her. *You're crazy if you think I'm going to even look for Smoking Mirror at all.* Aside from Michael, the only other god he truly feared deep in his essence was Smoking Mirror. Raphael was fooling himself if he thought he could defeat even a powerless Smoking Mirror.

And yet when he looked at Fiona and thought about what Smoking Mirror might do to her—what he'd done to so many humans before her—his stomach knotted painfully. Smoking Mirror could liberate his kind, but at what cost? Was it worth overthrowing the angelic tyranny just to replace it with the same thing under a different leader? Or even worse? Smoking Mirror hadn't been anyone's friend even before the angels came. *Lord Death was right; you didn't think this through at all.*

But Xolotl's master had also taught him the wisdom of playing both sides of the conflict, so he would find the other gods and see them returned to the Black Lake in Mictlan. Then they would be safe and ready to be resurrected again when the angels' time expired.

He just needed to be mindful to not get himself killed in the process. Or Fiona, for that matter.

She looked around, taking in the day's growing heat and the shimmer of mirages on the horizon. "Well, I don't know anything about tracking gods, so I guess you have to lead the way for me."

Xolotl wagged his tail. Leading the way was what Heaven had created him for.

Fiction by TL Morganfield

AZTEC WEST

The Hearts of Men
Death's Good Dog
The Dance of Destiny (*forthcoming 2015*)

THE BONE FLOWER TRILOGY

The Bone Flower Throne
The Bone Flower Queen
The Bone Flower Goddess (*forthcoming 2015*)

ONE WORLD ROMANCE

Fugitives of Fate

Join the mailing list at www.tlmorganfield.com to find out when new books and stories are available.

About the Author

T. L. Morganfield lives in Colorado with her husband and children. She's an alumna of the Clarion West Workshop and she graduated from Metropolitan State University with dual degrees in English and History. She reads and writes way too much about Aztec history and mythology, but it keeps her muse happy, which makes for a happy writer, so she has no plans of changing her ways.

Made in the USA
Columbia, SC
22 March 2025